# JOAN KOMLOSY

# CRACKING UP

Matador
9 De Montfort Mews
Leicester LE1 7FW, UK
Tel: (+44) 116 255 9311 / 9312
Email: books@troubador.co.uk
Web: www.troubador.co.uk/matador

ISBN 978 1906221 898

A Cataloguing-in-Publication (CIP) catalogue record for this
book is available from the British Library.

**Mixed Sources**
Product group from well-managed
forests and other controlled sources
www.fsc.org  Cert no. TT-COC-2082
© 1996 Forest Stewardship Council

Typeset in 11pt Stempel Garamond by Troubador Publishing Ltd, Leicester, UK
Printed in the UK by The Cromwell Press Ltd, Trowbridge, Wilts, UK

**Matador** is an imprint of Troubador Publishing Ltd

*In memory of the late (often) Kerry Juby*
*my friend and mentor*

# CHAPTER ONE

I've always thought it must be a nightmare to be a man, what with fighting in wars, going bald and having uncontrollable erections every five seconds (just not convenient when you have both hands full with children and shopping). However, since this morning, everything's changed. I now have a serious case of moustache envy. Overnight, cracks and crevices have appeared from nowhere on my upper lip. One minute I had perfect vitamin E-toned skin and the next I looked like an Australian bush person. Perhaps I'll change my name to Alice Springs? When the Californians have an earthquake, they say it's San Andreas' fault. In my case I say it's Dan Walters' fault as since splitting up with him five years ago, I've had nothing much to smile about. So they're not laughter lines. If I were a man I could grow a moustache and not only hide the disfigurement but also attract hordes of gorgeous women who have a thing about facial hair. As it is, my parched-earth look will repel every fanciable male in sight, not to mention the war-weary, balding, premature-ejaculating ones.

Cosmetic surgery is out. Not just because I couldn't afford it (after all I do live close to Harley Street and could at least save on the bus fare) but having seen the ghastly results in a television programme about ageing Hollywood stars – and by ageing I mean twenty-something – then I would need brain surgery as well. I could have Botox injections but do I really want frozen facial muscles *as well as* a frozen bank account? I think not.

My instinct was to pick up the 'phone and ring my mother who, at seventy, looks forty. I wished that I hadn't.

"Don't worry," she laughed. "When you reach the menopause you *will* more than likely grow a moustache."

1

I was digesting this piece of good news when she added, "And if you're wondering why *I* don't have one, it's because I shave daily!"

Life is gross.

The few relationships I've had recently have been nothing more than keeping my hand in, so to speak, as I've heard that if you don't have sex for a long period, you are likely to go off it completely. I'm almost off it completely as it is. Since the break-up, there's no-one I've really been that attracted to, apart from the actor James Woods (sexiest pock marks in the world). I was hoping to persuade an editor to commission me to do an in-depth interview with him but they've all said, "No-one knows him here and anyway, he's got bad skin." (This was, of course, pre the hit TV series *Shark*, when he was gorgeous, with youthful pock marks!)

That's how I met Dan. Not through his bad skin - although funnily enough he, too, had an acute acne-hangover problem – but through an interview. As a rock music reporter in the eighties, I interviewed everyone from present day icons like Tina Turner to has-beens like P J Proby. I always carried a tape recorder to parties as in one night I could sometimes get most of the rock news that I compiled for the weekly programme that I worked on. Invitations came thick and fast in those days, although I did realise that it wasn't my company particularly that was so sought after, but rather the publicity I might give the occasion. Anyway, amongst all the record company hype there were always one or two genuine invitations and one of these was to a party at the Polydor record company HQ. Keyboard player, Dan Walters, was there on his own. I'd only ever seen him with the rest of his band, usually paralytic – not a pretty sight. However, for once he was sober and he actually recognised me despite only having seen me from a horizontal position before. He gave me a warm hug and, surprisingly, I felt a quick rush. He was nice. Very nice.

"We should do an interview, Dan."

"I would like that. When? Tomorrow?" he asked eagerly.

When he arrived two days later, I knew he wouldn't be keeping his next appointment. Indeed, he cancelled everything for the rest of the day and spent it with me instead. And that was it. (Dan later said that when I opened the door, his heart went 'ding'. Guess what? So did mine.) He moved in with me and my youngest daughter Rebecca, a few weeks later. He sold his flat and with the proceeds we bought a weekend cottage in Hastings. We married after we'd been together for just three months as we were utterly and hopelessly besotted with each other. (Dan would wake me up several times every night to ask if I was alright – so sweet – although I would have been livid if anyone else had done that).

Our wedding reception was held at the studios where Dan had recorded many of his hits, so it was an appropriate venue. I made all the food and I can't believe I did it now when I look back. Dan and friends provided the live music. As there were over two hundred guests, my mother offered her services as a backup bouncer (having worked in a Magistrates Court for many years as a court usher, she was used to 'dealing with hooligans'). I tried to explain that it was a wedding party and not an illegal cockfight, but she was intent on doing it so there was no point in refusing her.

The first person she tried to bar was Dan's friend Sol. Already out of his tree, he kept falling onto her as he tried unsuccessfully to get past.

"Nana, don't do that," remonstrated my eldest daughter Laura. "He's a friend. He's lovely."

"Lovely?" echoed my mother in amazement. "He's drunk!"

Who wasn't? I sometimes think I was adopted at birth.

Sol was begrudgingly admitted to loud cheers and he ambled off to join Errol Brown in a duet (how surreal is that?) before slumping into a corner near the bar for the rest of the night. It certainly was a night to remember. The first person to ring and thank us the next day was Sol.

Dan, too, had a major drinking problem although it

didn't worry me over much at first as we were having such a great time. Pre-lunch champagne parties, post-lunch vodka parties and then on to the serious drinking until the early hours with assorted freeloaders and hangers-on.

I was very much in love with Dan by now, but I certainly would not have married him if he'd been at the peak of his career. I could not have accepted being apart for months on end whilst he toured the world. So we met at the right time, I thought. Not just a hiatus – punk rock had put paid to that – but a full stop. I still worked as a freelance reporter but that was fine because Dan knew everyone at the parties we went to. He also sat in on the interviews I did at home (so much easier than fighting for coveted studio time). He even stood in for me once when I lost my voice during an interview with Terence Trent D'Arby – and damned good it was, too.

I also had a Saturday stall in the Portobello Road antiques market. I'd had it for years and Dan was now eager to get involved. He had a natural flair for spotting a saleable item, although in the seven years that we were together he never got the hang of how much to pay for something. Over-paying results in either keeping the goods for ever or selling them at a loss.

Now that his fifteen minutes (or years in his case) was, to all intents and purposes, a thing of the past, antiques became a full-time pursuit. I eventually gave up my work (happily, I might add) as it was difficult to edit my tapes at home – Dan would sit opposite and blow kisses; lovely but distracting. (Friends thought it was nauseating but then I expect their partners only blew farts their way).

We travelled all over the country in search of stock, staying in delightful out-of-the-way and ludicrously cheap farmhouses and small hotels. We also went to our favourite city, Paris, on numerous occasions combining visits to flea markets and fairs with a few days holiday. It didn't always run smoothly though. On one occasion, Customs decided to give us the third degree and stripped the car down to something resembling a go-kart. They were obviously looking for drugs and, of course, found nothing as neither Dan nor I touched drugs. However, on the front seat I had accidentally left my bag which contained one or two items of jewellery that I had forgotten to declare at Customs as I was far too worried about how we were going to reassemble our car, (we were just handed the bits and told to get on with it) but no-one even looked at it. Far too obvious a place to stash drugs, I assume.

Another time, we left our wallet in a restaurant. It was our first night so we had all our stock money plus spending money in it. We got nearly back to the hotel – about twenty minutes away, when we realised what we'd done. We raced back and, against all the odds, the management had picked it up. So not only was Chez Quinson at 5, Place Etienne Pernet the best fish restaurant in Paris, but also the most honest, as far as we were concerned. In fact it was probably safer to leave our money (£4,000) on one of their tables than with the dubious looking security facilities at our hotel. And we weren't staying in a doss house!

Dan loved every aspect of his new 'career' so much that the night before Portobello he couldn't sleep for excitement. Determined to give up drinking, Dan went to AA meetings with Sol. The only trouble was they both needed a drink after the ordeal. After one particularly stressful meeting they made a beeline for the local fishmonger – that is, Sol did. Dan only realised where they were when his scotch on the rocks had bones in it. Sol bought the largest fish he could find and headed off in the direction of his (and Dan's) manager's office. Dan couldn't believe what Sol did next, so it must have been weird. He threw open the door and slung the fish at his open-mouthed manager then without a word shut the door and, giggling, headed for the nearest pub. They never did go to AA again. Dan did eventually give up through sheer will power and to this day, so I hear, has never touched another drop.

Dan's family was thrilled that he had 'settled down' at last and renounced his bad habits into the bargain. My family was also happy that I had 'found' Dan after years of on-off relationships. I had three daughters, Laura, Susie and Rebecca to my first husband, Patrick, but that marriage had ended some seventeen years previously and Patrick was now happily married to his third wife. We had remained friends over the years, so he too was pleased that I had met Dan (no more alimony!) And anyway their paths had crossed many times over the years as Patrick used to be a rock promoter and manager.

My mother was so proud of Dan that she took to browsing through the heavy metal section of her local record store and would feign surprise when she came across one of his records.

"Good heavens!" she would exclaim to the shop floor. "My son-in-law, Dan Walters!"

Rebecca also came in useful in public places.

"Rebecca," at foghorn pitch, "You know your stepfather, Dan Walters and your sisters, Laura and Susie who have danced at Covent Garden…"

I was always slightly peeved that I didn't get a name check. It could have worked.

"Rebecca, you know your mother, ex-Rag Queen, married to Dan Walters…"

Laura escaped these deranged outbursts as she was in Hollywood acting in TV soaps, (that is when she wasn't waiting on tables like all the other would-be actresses). If my mother had seen who was knocking on her door in those days, life would have been very complicated.

"Rebecca, your sister's seeing David Duchovny – who the heck does he think he is, anyway… It's a ridiculous series that he's in."

So you see, she wasn't always impressed.

Dan and I spent a lot of time at our cottage, going for long walks on the beach, playing snooker (we had picked up a magnificent full-size table that converted into a dining table should we wish to entertain in style) and pottering around the antiques shops along the south coast. Although we were inseparable, nevertheless we had petty rows like anyone else. Mostly, we would argue over band related incidents. Like the time Dan's manager sent us a joint birthday present (our birthdays were just a few days apart). Just what I'd always wanted – a policewoman stripogram! Or the time Dan gave our home address to some fans so that he could give them signed photographs. Not to mention records, stage gear and memorabilia. Well you would, wouldn't you, if they kept knocking on your door?

However, more serious issues were threatening as the eighties drew to a close. The great seventies revival was about to be unleashed. Dan's finest hour. How could he *not* revisit it? I understood, but it wasn't for me.

Arguments over the re-formation turned bitter and Dan eventually sought solace elsewhere. A fisherman's wife who worked in the bar of the local hotel, she was about my age and nondescript. I was disgusted. He could at least have picked a drop-dead gorgeous sexy young chick.

And so I left Dan.

# CHAPTER TWO

Dominic was game, "I'll have a go, but I doubt it will fit. It's not like a shoe, condoms don't come in half sizes."

He tried all five before giving up. "I told you. What happened to the other one, by the way?"

"It fit …Kieran. You've not done this before, have you?"

"What, had sex?"

"No, used a condom."

"Not really."

"And what does that mean, exactly?"

"OK, so I haven't. No-one's ever asked me to before."

I was shocked. "But you are thirty-four years old, you screw around. How do you know you've not got some horrible disease? Aids, more than likely."

"I'm fine. Don't be so paranoid. I don't go with slags."

"You are so stupid. You can't tell just by looking at someone whether they've got Aids or not – everyone knows that. And you *do* go out with slags. That one you were with on Friday has been examined – and I don't mean *cross-examined* – by every lawyer at Lincoln's Inn."

"I must admit I did probe her in depth. Look, don't worry, nothing will happen. I'll try them on again, they've stretched a bit now."

"Don't come near me!"

"I wasn't going to come *near* you, I was hoping to come *in* you."

"Go home, Dominic. I've suddenly noticed all your imperfections – especially your half-inch dick."

"It's half size, not half-inch", he said indignantly, tugging at the rapidly shrinking member. "Well, it is now. It's your fault. Do you always talk about Aids when you're about to have sex?"

"No, because no-one else's brains wear blue jeans. I mean it, Dominic. Go home."

"I can't. I'm too drunk. I can't remember where I live." Muttering about tying a guiding piece of string the next time to his knob (door) and my knocker (door), he lurched off into the night.

My daughter Susie first introduced me to Dominic. He'd done some conveyancing work for her and I needed a solicitor. He was, apparently, very witty and very cheap – just up my street (at the other end, in fact, so convenient as well). The only slight drawback was that he'd never handled a divorce case before but he thought it 'might be fun' and was 'game to have a go'. The alarm bells should have rung then.

Dominic woke me far too early the following morning.

"Great night", he chirruped, "But why was I in Clive's bed and not yours?"

"Because you had a shrinkage problem. Don't you remember?"

"At least I went through five condoms in one night. How many men can boast of that?"

I sighed. "You are pathetic. Are you *sure* you'll be able to get me divorced?"

"Meet me for lunch and we'll discuss it."

"But we've been discussing it for six months now. There's nothing else to say about the matter – unless you count the letter I've just got from Dan's solicitor saying that there is a billiard ball missing. How much will she charge him for writing that? £150? For a tenner I could buy an antique *ivory* one. Perhaps I will, and send it to her. Through her window. No wonder this divorce is taking so long – all this pedantic rubbish."

I was on Legal Aid but Dan was obviously paying through the nose as it was now three years since proceedings had begun. I had been with a couple of other solicitors before Dominic came on the scene and both had started off enthusiastically but had shunted me on to a back burner when more lucrative cases came their way. Fortunately, Dominic didn't have to do this as conveyancing kept his bank balance healthy.

The wine bar was just around the corner and, as Locals go, was quite acceptable. But it was always the same routine and today was no exception. Pretty girl walks in, Dominic stiffens (I toy with pulling out the emergency condom from my purse), I sigh, he tears himself away from the heavenly vision just long enough to explain that it's "Dave, an old school friend. Ooh, he's had a sex change!"

This was very funny the first few times, but it must have been a bloody big school.

"I'm bored with you trying to pick up girls in pubs, especially when you're supposed to be with me. It's very rude."

Dominic laughed guiltily. "I don't pick up girls in pubs. Do you think I go to the bar and ask for a pint of lager, a packet of crisps and that bird in the corner?"

The age gap only slightly bothered me (if I'd been a child bride, I could have been his mother). However, his mental age – fifteen – didn't bother me at all. In fact, that's definitely what attracted me. But I *was* bored with his rituals. As my mother would say of him, 'He's a good turn but he's on too long'. I certainly wasn't jealous. Also, my new-found singledom meant that Dominic was not going to be the only eligible male trying on my condoms for size.

However, taking the plunge again hadn't been easy.

Dan and I had written a book together about the amusing times we had at the various antiques fairs that we did four times a year at showgrounds around the country. As many of the other exhibitors featured in it, we were guaranteed a few sales. This was now post-Dan so I had to take any praise/flak on my own. A name check sure brings out the prima donna in some people. Here's an example:

A woman in her seventies comes to the stand. She smells of stale urine and *Poison* – the latter being slightly more obnoxious than the urine.

"What's that?" she asks in a posh voice, pointing to a Victorian plaque. "Is it wood? I can't see because I'm certified blind. How much is it? And what are those birds on that mirror?"

I was about to say that the birds were actually cows.

"I mean, are they robins or pheasants…what are they?" she continues impatiently. "How much is it, anyway? Give me a bargain on the two."

Fifty pounds, apparently, is a bargain.

"Yes, I'll have them. Now I only have two cheques left and I have to pay someone else so can you keep them until next week?"

Thankfully, I explain that we would be in London and we wouldn't have wanted a cheque anyway. Normally I would not mind but in the circumstances I was quite keen for her to take her odours somewhere else.

"Then I will have them next week. I live in London. Could you deliver them?"

Dan says we can. He has no sense of smell after a heavy cold so my glaring look just confuses him.

"I live in Earls Court. You probably have to go past there."

"No."

"I'm doing up another floor in my house," she continues. "My housekeeper lives on one floor and I have the top floor. It's very untidy but I love beautiful things and I'm going to have a beautiful room for strangers to visit and for well-to-do people to stay. That's if I live long enough. I've been told I'll go before my eyesight packs up completely."

Her departing shot was, "I'll give you a bottle of wine and your petrol money."

I would have preferred a clothes peg.

Now, is that offensive or not? I say anyone who calls their perfume (sic) 'Poison' is a legitimate target.

I had tried to do the stands on my own after the split but it had been a nightmare. I don't drive (I know, pathetic) so it was the night bus to King's Cross and then the milk train to wherever. With four bags of stock. How lace tablecloths and a few bits of jewellery can turn into the equivalent of four bags of coal is one of those unfathomable mysteries. Something else I've noticed about coal – and this really is a brain-teaser –

the bags feel heavier sometimes on the return journey despite having sold at least forty per cent of the contents. Cleverclogs are going to say it's because I'm tired after the fair and although the bags are of course lighter, they just *feel* heavier on my wilting frame. Well, no. My frame is already wilting at three in the morning when I start the journey. And the problem doesn't end there. Two days is a long time to man a stand on one's own so, invariably, neighbours are asked to keep an eye whilst one dashes to the loo. There is always a queue, so the dash turns into a fifteen minute wait and by the time you return, your neighbours have probably forgotten that they are supposed to be watching your stock, and are engaged with a customer of their own.

"Where's that ten thousand pound diamond ring?" You can almost hear the heart racing. "Only joking. Thanks for looking after my stall."

The answer was to share with a friend. Emma lives nearby and sells similar things, so at least the stall wouldn't look crazy. (I've seen dealers with fine porcelain sharing with someone who sells petrol pump globes). It worked well – a bit cramped, but a small price to pay. On the way back to London after our first fair together, we stopped for a welcome break at a *Little Chef* (we hadn't fancied stopping for a little chef at a *Welcome Break*) and as we were waiting at the checkout to pay, a bloke got out of his seat and came over to us.

"Did you write that book about the Fair?" he asked me. I nodded, but how had he recognised me? The cover photo looked nothing like I looked at that moment, as I was obviously not covered in mud with bird's nest hair. It was quite insulting that he should think we were the same person. I instinctively didn't like him.

"It kept me awake all night. I really enjoyed it."

"Oh, thanks. So, do you always do this fair? I've never seen you before."

"I've seen you."

Emma nudged me in the ribs. "I'll wait for you outside."

"I'm coming now," I said, scooping up my change.

"My name's Luke, I have a stall at Camden Lock. Why don't you come and have breakfast with me on Sunday?"

"Oh, I can't. But thanks anyway. Some other time."

Emma was thrilled for me. "Lily, he's gorgeous, you *must* meet him."

"I didn't think he *was* gorgeous and I'm *not* going to meet him. Apart from that, he's far too young." If and when I did start dating again, I wanted my partner to be at least as old as my eldest daughter and I didn't think this one was.

"That doesn't matter. You're only going to have sex with him for goodness sake, you're not going to marry him."

Although Emma was a good deal older than I and had never been married, she was very broad-minded. In her younger days she had been an exotic showgirl and dancer so that probably accounted for it

I thought about Luke now and again over the next few weeks and one Sunday, I decided to take up his offer of breakfast. Emma was right. He *was* gorgeous. So he was going to be the first man on my road to recovery. Nevertheless, flirting with a stranger felt very weird, childishly thrilling. He was twenty-four. Ridiculous. When I told him my age he was amused.

"You're older than my mother." Seeing my pained expression, he went on, "But I don't mind. I like it."

So he had an Oedipus complex and no doubt was hoping I'd show him a few tricks. The younger man and older woman thing. It was *so* not what I wanted. But then what did I want? Easy. The seventies revival to have been the sixties revival instead.

He shunned the condom I had thoughtfully prepared, on the grounds that he would break out in swellings. I said one swelling would be fine by me. Like most married couples, Dan and I never used condoms. After all, there was no need as we were joined at the hip, according to our friends, so a bit on the side would have been just that. And three's a crowd. I'd dismissed Dan's previous rock star lifestyle simply because he told me that the groupie thing had never appealed to him and, as Samuel Johnson said, 'Love is the wisdom of the fool and the folly of the wise.' However, Luke was a different kettle of fish. I didn't know anything about his previous sexual partners so the next time we were facing each other (missionary position), I feebly attempted to bring up the subject again.

"I've got green ones."

Not missing a stroke, he replied, "I – don't – use - them – Lily."

"If we do this again, you're going to have to," I counterpointed.

"Why, do you think you could get pregnant at your age?

"Thanks for that and yes, I probably could, but that's not the point. There are some horrible diseases around these days."

"Don't worry, I haven't got anything and I'm sure you haven't."

We carried on but I'd lost interest after that confident exchange and wished he'd hurry up as I now couldn't wait to fake my orgasm.

I decided not to see Luke again after discussing his aversion to contraceptives with a friend who was one of the country's leading HIV and Aids specialists. I was told in no uncertain terms that not only must I see that my partner wore top quality sheaths ('and always check the sell-by dates') but that I should also use *oral* protectives. What the fuck were they, I wondered? I didn't know anyone who used them. They turned out to be rubber things the size of plates, shaped like inverted dummies. So what happens if this 'comforter' gets stuck in your throat? I'll just have to give up oral sex (not too difficult) and that's all there is to it. I know it won't go down well – it won't go down at all in fact, but sex starts at the shoulders from now on.

# CHAPTER THREE

Money was becoming a problem as Dan wasn't helping with the bills. Indeed, he rather hoped I would send him part of the proceeds from Portobello. In normal circumstances, I probably would have done but I think his record royalties had the edge on profits from junk shop tat. Because that's what I was reduced to buying after I'd sold off the good stuff in order to pay my rent, etc. When that money ran out, I had no alternative but to sign on.

I have been lucky in that I've led a relatively charmed life so I accepted that it was my turn for a bit of grief, but I'd not bargained for such humiliation and frustration as well. Now I'm not stupid but those DSS forms are so confusing – even the officer on duty admitted that he had never come across anyone who filled them in correctly first time. I know the intention is to deter would-be defrauders but genuine cases don't need this nightmare, their lives are wretched enough. The next stage involved filling in more forms at another branch. This time my mother accompanied me. Tripping over pit bull terriers (unmuzzled), fractious children and *Special Brew* cans, (whatever happened to meths bottles?) we fought our way to the ticket machine. I drew number 46, which meant there were thirty-eight people before me. I know; I couldn't work it out either. Nearly an hour later, unbelievably, only four people had been seen. Meanwhile my mother had asked the man next to her if he could read.

"It says 'No Smoking', so please put it out."

He blew a stream of smoke in her face defiantly and replied, "Everyone else is smoking."

She said she would see about that and strode over to the

bullet-proof booth. "Where's the manager, please. This lot can't read," she said, gesticulating at the crowd.

Without looking up the young girl said, "Go back to your seat and wait your turn."

Incensed, my mother replied, "I'm not in the queue."

"Then get in it instead of trying to push in."

"How dare you speak to me like that – a bit of a kid! Fetch the manager at once." My mother's outrage fell on deaf ears. The bit of a kid merely continued writing. By now, the whole room was enthralled. A young bloke behind said to his mate, "This is better than Covent Garden, much more entertaining."

I would have been embarrassed in normal circumstances, but it was all so surreal that it simply didn't matter. No manager was forthcoming so I dragged my protesting mother out into the street. "I'll come back tomorrow and I'll be here first thing to avoid all that," I told her.

The next day I was there – minus my mother – twenty minutes before the doors opened. Ahead of me was an unshaven black man who, on closer inspection, turned out to be white – just in need of a damned good wash. He was knocking back a can of SB and chain smoking (at least the DSS must pay well these days). He was joined by another heavily inebriated dosser and together they swayed unsteadily, swigging and inhaling two inches away from my face. I couldn't move back because the queue had grown and everyone was jam-packed up against each other in their urgency to get inside the place. More derelicts were joining the original one ahead of me, cadging cigarettes and projecting a strange camaraderie. Fearing I would be trapped again in that dreadful place, I saw red.

"Get to the back of the queue," I screamed, any compassion I'd been feeling, now lost. Amazingly, they did, politely reassuring me that they were not intending to push in. After that it was pretty straight forward and I was at the bullet-proof window by 9.05 a.m.

"A packet of cigarettes and two cans of lager, please."

The young officer grinned. "I know what you mean." He was sympathetic and helped me to fill in the new forms. I walked out, head held high, little dreaming I would be back there in a few weeks when my papers 'got lost in the system'. Because my husband was a relatively famous rock star, I was given the third degree. I was shuttled back and forth between different offices for weeks until it was reluctantly accepted that Dan was not keeping me in the style to which I'd grown accustomed.

Attending the DSS offices once a fortnight was a depressing affair. Already demoralised, this was a constant reminder that you were now at the bottom of the heap, although the signing-on office was more like the lounge of a Grade Two hotel – more your Martini set. In fact a sure sign of those recession-hit times, the assignees were smart on the whole. You could always spot a new recruit, (best clobber, new haircut, nervous cough and shades) and for some reason they nearly always carried copies of *The Independent*.

Dark days indeed. I was missing Dan dreadfully, my children had left home (and who could blame them in the circumstances? I was not fun to be around), and my landlords had started to give me a hard time. The block where I lived had recently changed hands and the new owners wanted to sell the flats once the leases came up for renewal. A refurbishment programme was underway (this was to blight my life for the next few years) and statutory tenants, of which I was one, were approached with varying highly secretive offers to leave. As my offer was so derisory I had no problem in turning it down, expecting a more realistic one to follow. The landlords had other ideas, however - a sort of 'Let's smoke her out' plan – and it wasn't long before the first match was lit.

Meanwhile, I needed to get out of this downward spiral quickly so I rang a couple of friends at Capital radio, but they were unable to help as things had become much more in-house and there was now nothing for freelances. I got in touch with LBC and one of the producers offered me some work, but like all independent radio stations – apart from Capital – there was no money, so I was lucky to receive around £30 per interview. (I know people who do actually work for nothing just to keep their CV up to date). I also had to edit the tapes, so each interview could take up to two days, especially if I had to travel to the interviewee. The producer started getting creative and suggested adding music at the beginning and end – lots of fading in and out.

The trouble was I had never used studio editing units (I had always edited on my UHER tape recorder), but didn't want to tell the producer in case he knew someone who could. So I rang Marsha Brendon, one of my ex-producers, and she offered to come to the studio when my producer, John, wasn't there and show me how to do it. Now, I'm a Luddite – and not proud of it – but there it is. I simply don't adapt easily to new technology. Not that I have anything against it in principle (so I suppose I'm not a Luddite in the true sense), but I'm a slow learner. However, once I do get the hang of things, I'm pretty damned good. In fact, editing on a UHER was far from easy (and I thought it was only me in the beginning), but I could do almost anything. For example, I once bumped into Isaac Hayes coming out of the lavatory at the Camden Palace club, so I thrust my ever ready microphone in his face and asked him what he was currently up to. He could have said 'Putting my dick away, you Moron', but he didn't, he was charm itself. Later, editing the interview, the background noises became all too apparent as flushing lavatories and slamming doors interspersed throughout.

The producer and the presenter were used to my background noises, so much so that Roger would ask the listeners sometimes to guess where the interview had taken place (the runway at Heathrow was a favourite). However, these particular noises masked the questions. In a way it was fortuitous as I could ask my questions again, but I couldn't have asked Mr. Hayes as he was no doubt zipping up his trousers on the other side of the world by now. Caesar's

Palace, maybe. The problem would be how to make it sound authentic. I tuned in my three radios to three different talk programmes, put the Clash and the Sex Pistols on in different rooms at full blast and stuck a Motorhead concert on the video. Perfect, Camden Palace re-created in my flat (no need to go out again, ever). I edited in the relevant bits and not one person noticed when the interview was broadcast the following Sunday, although I did half expect Sol to ring to say that he was surprised he'd been gigging at Camden Palace as he thought he was at an AA meeting with Dan.

Nevertheless the wizardry was confined to my skills on the UHER and not to a thing covered in spools and knobs with daunting instructions. As I didn't want Marsha to know that I hadn't in fact really absorbed all the complicated moves – and I couldn't expect her to do it for me every week – I had no choice but to quit on the grounds that something better had come up unexpectedly. At least the DSS paid better.

Yet again, my daughter Susie came to my rescue. She had a friend who was starting a lifestyle magazine, so she mentioned me to him. He liked the idea of a music column so I became a regular contributor until the magazine folded ten months later. Although the money was crap, Nathan's wonderful parties more than made up for it. They were held in his fabulous Chelsea penthouse. (Susie lived in a doll's house opposite, so there was no problem staggering back to her place afterwards.)

Nathan and his wife Serena owned an hotel in Suffolk. This imposing manor, Uplands Hall, was furnished with eye-catching antiques from floor to ceiling. It would have been so easy to stuff one's *Louis Vuitton* (or Poundstretcher luggage in my case) with rare bronzes, first editions and gold snuff boxes instead of the usual towels and complimentary shower-cap, but amazingly no-one ever did. Nathan said the only thing that had ever walked was a silver match case worth thirty quid, and he wasn't sure that he hadn't simply misplaced it.

Nathan was always coming up with schemes to have fun and maybe make some money as well. Some worked but most didn't as the fun side always got in the way of the money side. One of the projects was a luxury dinner dating agency. The dinners would be held once a month at Uplands, a perfect setting for single, eligible and rich clients. The first event needed padding out as it was a rushed affair (Nathan always wanted to road-test his ideas immediately), so Susie and I were recruited to swell the disappointingly low female bookings. Susie was married but her husband, Gerry, didn't mind her going so long as she promised not to give her real 'phone number to anyone (she couldn't say she was married as we were supposed to be single, so faking it was the only way to maintain the deception).

We set off in a light-hearted, giggly mood. I was feeling happier about dating now although I couldn't imagine doing it this way for real as it felt last resort-ish and I was far from that stage. Susie is a very fast driver, something that has always unnerved me as not only am I a non-driver, but also a back-seat driver so when a lorry with its mile-long trailer swinging wildly from side to side cut us up, I blessed the day my daughter had never heeded my advice on road safety. We escaped death by a millimetre, according to Susie.

Nathan had given us a double suite for our efforts and this went a long way towards compensating for the prospect of being chatted up by losers and saddos – albeit wealthy ones. We arrived early so it was great to soak in the vast nineteenth-century tubs, watching swans glide by on the lake below and sipping champagne, thoughtfully placed at just the right angle for reaching whilst semi-supine. We got ready like excited teenagers despite our silly, patronising speculations.

There must have been about forty people already gathered in the library when we made our grand entrances. I know it's immodest to blow one's own trumpet but we did look great. Susie, a young Kylie Minogue look-alike in her little black number (which had probably turned her bank account into a little red number) and me in my charity shop bargain of the century, a vintage *Christian Dior* sequinned cocktail dress. We draped ourselves around a marble column, sipping yet another glass of champagne, preparing ourselves for the onslaught. By the end of our fourth glass we realised with horror that no-one was even looking at us, let alone swooning at our beautifully pedicured feet. Everyone was either in a group or having an animated one-to-one conversation. Susie whispered, "I want to die."

I said, "I'm glad this is a recent desire. Two hours earlier and you'd have got your wish."

Finally, one ghastly little man came over and announced, "Well, this lot might be frightened to come over but someone's got to break the ice. I'm Julian."

We could have kissed him – I think we probably did, we were so grateful. But what did he mean by 'frightened' of us?

"Well, you do look like the untouchables. Aloof women, however attractive – and may I say you are very, *very* attractive, (creep) scare us chaps. We think you are going to reject us big time."

Too right, Matey. But not just yet. We needed him as a temporary decoy and sure enough, it wasn't long before Clarence, George and Seymour were trying out their chat-up lines on us, gems such as 'Would you like to come here often – I can afford to bring you."

At dinner the men had to shift two places to their right after each course, thus ensuring that everyone had a chance to make more than just eye contact. Over Celery Sorbet and Stilton Mousse, I nodded off as the Rt. Hon. Somebody Goring (or was that Boring?) held forth (no wonder he was single) and to my left, John the electrician (how did he get in?) was sadly just as mind-blowingly dull. The waiter took forever to clear the plates so there was nothing for it but to learn how to change a fuse – fractionally more interesting than Snoring's monologue about falling into the Thames at the Henley Regatta.

"Amazing," I said, feigning bemusement. "And you're still wet."

My next two were a great improvement. Farmer Duncan from up the road, something of an oddball but drily amusing. His twin brother, Farmer James was also there, one course away from Susie who had ice-breaker Julian on one side and a man with a poor head of hair on the other. Laurence, a ski instructor of thirty-five was the youngest there, incredibly good-looking and very amusing.

"What on earth are you doing here? Surely you have girls falling over themselves – forgive the pun – to date you?"

"I could say the same about you and your sister."

Candlelight is very flattering and he was probably a bit snowblind to boot. He went on, "I thought it would be fun. Jack, over there, suggested it, so why not?" Then tongue-in-cheek, he added, "I never go out with piste women."

I took a swig of tap water, hmm lovely, before confessing that my sister and I were just helping out – but I at least was willing to go with the flow. Floe even.

Duncan, by way of explaining the vast number of pencils that he had in his pocket, said he was very, very rich.

"I like pencils. I can't go in a shop without buying a bunch."

I assumed that was why he wasn't married – women just didn't get off on pencils.

"No, it's because I don't want some woman getting her hands on all my money."

I liked Duncan a lot. Marks out of ten? 2HB.

"Mummy!" I tried to ignore Susie's flagrant breaking of the rules, but Laurence intervened.

"Lily, your sister wants you."

Well, that was that, I presumed. I wouldn't be sliding down his bedpost now.

"I knew anyway," he laughed.

"But you referred to her as my sister."

"I was just going along with it. It was funny. Sweet."

I was intrigued. "But how *did* you know?" Fingers crossed he wouldn't say 'your seventies revival fixation'.

"She's been calling you Mummy all night."

"Has she?" I was genuinely amazed. But then she had called me that for twenty-three years so it was only natural for us to slip out of our new characters now and again.

The men were asked to move again but our section of the table protested as we were all getting on so well. However, Nathan was having none of it. Fair enough, but as I wasn't interested in anyone else but Laurence now, the rest of the meal passed in a haze as I needed something a bit stronger than water to get me through it. Most people were well tanked by the time we hit the dance floor – I did so literally, bruising my coccyx badly. Nevertheless I insisted that Laurence and I should play snooker as I was the champion of Hastings. I missed every ball – not surprising as I couldn't even see the table, never mind aim a cue.

I woke up the next morning, predictably by myself, Susie in the adjoining room (also by herself, Gerry). I was simply grateful I hadn't got to test the lead in Farmer Duncan's pencil. I found Laurence's card in my bag later but to this day I haven't dared to ring him.

The match-making scheme was to prove a short-lived affair as it wasn't financially viable in the end. The magazine folded about the same time as Nathan had became bored with the long hours. He had made his millions in the City and his investments in property were successful, so he could afford to indulge his whims.

Until the next time then, Nathan. You've got my number.

# CHAPTER FOUR

Before the builders moved in and turned where I lived into a building site (for the next four years), nothing much had changed since it was built at the turn of the century. The architect who designed the block must have had a penchant for urinals as every one of my basement flat windows looks out on to an eight foot wall of white tiles. I keep expecting to see a row of men out there. It's particularly confusing when it rains.

The flat itself is quite grand, situated near Regents Park in one of those turn of the century mansion blocks, where rooms were far more generously proportioned than the matchbox eyesores of today. It's a mixed bag of tenants, all nationalities – a robust Russian child used to tear about above my flat. I've had to complain several times to the child's parents as pictures have gone crooked whilst lights visibly shook. (It must be a first to have a red *over* a bed).

Now, I know that boys will be boys but I would rather he practised his rugby tackles somewhere else (preferably Moscow), instead of over my head at midnight. Once when his parents were away, understandably, a midnight romp with only an au pair to contend with was a must. Only my mother didn't see it that way. Here on one of her regular visits, she had just gone to bed when the terrible thundering started. I said I would complain, but she insisted on sorting it out. As I have already mentioned, my mother used to work at a Magistrates Court and simply can't get out of the habit. She offers her services all over the place, like last Christmas, when she decided to have a walk through Soho at the late (for a grandmother) hour of 10 pm to 'see the sights'. Coming across a policeman struggling with a bloody-nosed drinking dive reject, she flashed her Court ID card (she no doubt saw it as a flexi-Victoria Cross) and offered her assistance. He gratefully handed the man over to her whilst he adjusted his uniform and had a breather. So a nine-year old terror represented no threat.

Scary ID card in hand, she was halfway to the door when there was a huge explosion in the kitchen. We both thought that the neighbours had put a brick through the window. What had in fact happened was that the glass light shade had exploded due to the vibrations on its hot metal plate – a direct result of the overhead clog dancing. Well, that was all she needed because she was on the 'phone to the police before I could stop her. She really does like the company of policemen but this thinly veiled guise to get one or two round here so that she could tell them that she'd called the 'Ripper' into court was too much. I was so embarrassed when a James Woods look-alike turned up twenty minutes later. He was happy to leave the football hooligans in Trafalgar Square for a bit, he said, as he was getting his head kicked in, so my mother had inadvertently done him a favour. He'd forgotten his notebook so I gave him some paper but when I also offered him a pen he feigned indignation. "I do have a pen, I am a policeman, you know."

My mother filled him in on her years in court and he actually seemed interested. He learnt that she had called Peter Sutcliffe into court once on a traffic offence, eighteen months before he was nailed as the 'Yorkshire Ripper'. My mother knew all the prostitutes and drunks by name as they were in court regularly. The old drunks used to shout, "We love you, Big Tits!" She took it all in good humour – what else could she do, she did have big tits.

Obviously her work was fascinating but probably the most thrilling part of it – Rippers aside – was when someone whom she knew came into court. I always got a 'phone call afterwards, particularly if the someone was respectable and a pillar of society.

"Ooh, Lily love, you'll never guess who I had in court today."

"David Dimbleby?"

"Don't be silly. John Woodhead."

"Never heard of him."

Yes you have. Well you went to school with him."

"I'm sorry, Mother, but I probably know him as Pinocchio."

"You do say some ridiculous things."

Wood head, wooden headed doll – Pinocchio?"

The day my mother retired was a sad day all round as she was very popular with everyone, particularly the 'coppers', both male and female and of course, she loved her job.

PC James Woods eventually said he had to go back to the Doc Martens and thanked us for a thoroughly enjoyable evening. I reminded him gently of the true purpose of his visit and he said he would note our complaint even though it was an environmental issue.

Shortly after the light incident, the Russians left as their lease had expired and the landlords were not renewing unless they had to, as tarting up the flats and selling them was now the name of the game. When the entrance hall had its makeover, I couldn't believe that the wonderful elegant wood panelling and the wrought iron Edwardian lift were ripped out and replaced with hideous eyesores, not to mention the reproduction furniture and fake dado. If this was meant to attract classy Arabs, then it was way off track – more your Baghdado. But if I'd only known what I would be in for over the next few months, I wouldn't have been so 'bolshie' to the neighbours. But then again, they were no comrades of mine.

The Kanga drills moved in on day one and didn't leave until nine months later. The noise and vibrations were so overpowering that the landlords had to offer me the use of an empty flat in the block. However, that was short-lived as builders were ready to move in there as well, so three weeks later I was back in my hell-hole trying to write a feature for *My Weekly*, a homely magazine read, no doubt, in noise-free zones. It was impossible to concentrate so I had to write at night (too tired, usually) or go in the park. I tried the library, but oddly enough that was noisy as well, all that 'shushing' and scraping of chairs.

The first flood was relatively minor. Nevertheless, a wall in a bedroom was running with water and cracks had appeared as a result. The carpet, of course, was sodden. Not too bad, then. The next one wasn't so good. I'd stayed out all day as usual as I didn't want to hear even thirty seconds of drilling. The men usually knocked off at 5.30 pm but were scheduled to work until 6 pm (and the way they worked that Kanga, the bastards were bound to go the course one of these days), so I'd hung around until the coast was clear. When I got in, water was pouring through the ceiling, my favourite oil painting ruined, a soaked carpet again and my grand piano thoroughly splashed. The builders had left with the key so it was another two hours before the porters could get in to turn off the tap that had 'inadvertently' been left on in a blocked up bath. However, pissed off though I felt, I was determined not to be flushed out. This tenant was not for quitting.

A few weeks later I was up north visiting my mother when Rebecca rang urging me to return at once as the ceiling in the hall had come down and water was pouring in. With the help of the head porter she had managed to rescue my rare twelve-seater Art Deco table which had been strewn with debris and worrying pools of water. The fitted carpet was beyond salvage and had been taken up, leaving the unsightly concrete floor exposed. Although the landlords had to ultimately acknowledge responsibility, they took weeks making good as apportioning blame was nigh on impossible. The contractors had sub-contracted and they in turn had sub-contracted until confusion reigned. As far as I was concerned, the landlords hired the contractor and what happened afterwards was irrelevant.

I had met Dominic by this time and he wrote one or two letters to back up my claims. Meanwhile I had to put up with a squalid and depressing flat whilst various foremen, builders and nosey parkers working in other flats trampled through, making notes and facile comments every day for two weeks.

The landlords' usual excuses were that the building hadn't been renovated since it was built, around 1900, so things were bound to go wrong with the ancient plumbing system. There would be two more on a much lesser scale but by now it was grist for the mill. However, the leak in the bathroom, which *was* due to the ancient plumbing in *my* flat was a different kind of experience. But more of that later.

Desperate to get away from the heavy weather indoors, a magazine ad caught my eye. It was for a five day songwriters' workshop near Oxford in two weeks time. I didn't stop to think. I picked up the 'phone and rang the number. I was lucky, there had been a cancellation, so I was booked onto the course. I felt elated. After all the negative things that were going on in my life, this would be positive, a challenge and, hopefully, rewarding as there is always something new to learn.

I *am* a songwriter although I haven't written anything since I split with Dan, as I have felt totally uninspired. (I did write one heartrending lament, lots of crashing B flat minor chords and angst-ridden lyrics – music to cut your wrists to). However, I used to churn them out regularly and can proudly claim that one went into the charts in the seventies. Admittedly it was in the now defunct *Record Mirror's* Soul Chart, but still, it was a start.

Whitegates Farm was a well-known and successful venue for writing courses run by the owners, Polly and Sam. Sam had been a successful writer in the seventies but was more interested in running the courses and the farm now. There were nine of us, four men and five women of all ages and backgrounds, so a mixed bag. I felt an instant rapport with two of them, Annette Bryan and Callum. (Callum reminded me of a handsome Nick Hornby – sorry Mr. Hornby). The others I could take or leave although I would become fond of them all in an 'air raid shelter-ish' sort of way.

I had decided not to tell anyone why I was really there, and I didn't want to mention Dan even though I knew Sam would know him. It could prejudice judgement of my work one way or another.

I was quite shocked to find that I would be sharing a room as I've never shared a room with a stranger before. Well I have, but it's been with a man. And of my choosing. I drew the short straw – and the fattest. I will call her Kaftan to spare her blushes as I'm going to be rude about her (she did have an equally daft name, by the way). We had our own huge bathroom which was good news, particularly as we would be doing our homework in our rooms and there was no way I could write in front of someone, so I could at least sit there. Unless she peed a lot.

Polly was a great cook and we had a really enjoyable first evening (the only one, apart from the last, that I would have). Kaftan and I went 'home' together as I wanted to check out her habits. What she did in the privacy of the bathroom didn't bother me (so long as I couldn't hear it) but what she did in front of me did. Now, call me unreasonable, but going to bed in thirty bangles (fifteen on each arm) jingling and jangling with every twitch and turn, is anti-social. I put up with it for two nights and on the third I asked her – nicely – to remove them. She said she couldn't as she had water retention. Steak and kidney pie retention, more like. I know I'm a noise freak – thanks to the Kangas – but, really. How could a bangle jangler have music in her soul? Why was she on this course I wondered? Indeed, she'd been on other courses of Sam's, so she can't have been totally without rhythm or Sam wouldn't, I suspect, have put up with it. After all, he didn't seem to be in it for the money. I would soon be enlightened. Kaftan was one of the three who only wrote lyrics (nothing wrong with that – where would George have been without Ira, one can wonder?) and perfect pitch is not a prerequisite to producing a masterly lyric. Perhaps she will one day. Perhaps she already has – Walk Like An Egyptian – in a Kaftan, by the Bangles?

Sam met us all separately the next day to discuss how the week would pan out and to establish what we hoped to achieve by the end of it. He was very unassuming which made the more nervous amongst us visibly relieved. He didn't muck about though, he gave us our first assignment there and then. I'd never written a song in just four hours before – because that's how long we had before he wanted to hear how we were shaping up, something that was at least the foundation of the theme he'd set.

I thought it would be interesting to have a go. Unfortunately, I was the only one who wrote on the piano. The other five played guitar and the only piano was in the room where Sam held his one-to-ones (and those took nearly all day). And so it transpired that I would manage a mere two hours a day (I can't write in my head, I *need* a keyboard) whilst the others had seven or eight so they could be wandering minstrels serenading the chickens, perched on tractors or rolling in the hay (rock 'n' rolling, that is).

That first day, I admit I cheated. I re-wrote the lyrics to one of my previous songs which hadn't been published so no-one had heard it before. This would get me through the first appraisal (which now appeared to be set for the following day) as it wasn't bad and would look like a respectable stab, given only two hours. Until I knew what the competition was (not that we were competing), I couldn't risk making a fool of myself.

Dinner that night was even more of an occasion as we excitedly discussed the task set us and how we were progressing. The palpable relief that we could now relax and enjoy the friendly proximity of Sam over *lobster bisque* and Polly's own delicious organic chicken (I assumed it had been 'sung' to death that morning).

"Right, if we could retire to the sitting room now," said Sam languorously, "We'll have coffee first."

First? It sounded ominous. What came after 'first', I wondered? There was no-one I fancied so if an orgy was planned to loosen us up a bit (Well, *I* don't know what goes on at these writing courses), I'd have to go home.

"I'd like to hear what you've written."

Only later did I realise that when he said 'I', he meant the republican 'I', as in the royal 'We'. How cruel to lull us into such a false sense of security over dinner, putting us at ease to the point where I'd draped my legs over my next door neighbour, Callum, in a show of relaxed mateyness. Odd how I didn't mind the thought of playing my song in private to a successful songwriter, but to demonstrate it in front of a bunch of fellow would-be's turned me into a quaking wreck. Annette was also freaked as she, too, hadn't anticipated the public show of her talents. In fact, she was one of the best writers, Jack Morley perhaps having the edge on her, in my opinion. She was certainly the best singer, but far too modest to believe this.

I wanted to get it over with so I begged to go first. At least I had my back to everyone. I got through a verse and a chorus thankfully without a hitch. Relieved, I said to Sam, "And so on and so forth."

"Well, let's hear the rest of it, then."

Horror of horrors. I didn't feel at all confident with the new lyrics and was convinced he would instinctively know that I had cheated. Somehow I got through the rest of it – damn, I shouldn't have finished it in one go – and slunk back to my seat to polite applause. But worse was to come. Sam went round the group asking each one for their comments. Everyone was very kind – not a bit constructive as they should have been, but it was the first night and everyone was nervous now, so it was a bit of an insurance policy. Sam too was surprisingly kind but he did say I needed to work more on my lyrics as they didn't match the mood of the music in parts.

I woke up the next morning with a sense of foreboding. I would have to go through yesterday's nightmare all over again and this time it would be even worse as I would have to actually compose something from scratch. I was determined not to re-hash anything else but the pressure felt enormous. I joined Annette for breakfast. She was having similar qualms in that her lack of confidence in her ability – despite having played in front of audiences in the past as a professional singer/songwriter – was making her wonder if she'd done the right thing in coming on the course. We both said we'd give it a go but were not sure we'd last the week. Annette came from a small village in Shropshire and was married with two children. Her husband Derek had taken a week off school (he was a maths teacher) to look after them. I really did like her and, indeed, had it not been for her pep talks and encouragement, I would definitely have done a runner.

It wasn't that the storylines Sam set us were difficult in themselves, it was simply lack of time, for me, to develop the ideas in anything other than a rudimentary piss-poor way. One of the chaps only had one melody – but didn't know it – and would change the lyrics depending on the day's exercise. Despite us all being able to hum each 'new'song, the penny never dropped. Sam wisely concentrated on the lyrics as they were after all the main event, and by the end of the week he had honed them into expressions of such vibrancy and depth that the one tune somehow sounded different each time. That was another reason to stay. Sam's teaching skills. Despite the permanently agitated state I was in, he was able to bring out the best in me and although I wasn't sitting in on the other sessions, it was obvious from their progress – without exception – that Sam had fine-tuned whatever talent was there. He really does have a remarkable instinctive teaching ability.

If I hadn't been so fearful, I would have enjoyed it so much, but at least I would look back fondly in hindsight. As it was, there were moments of pleasure that got me through each day. Callum was an actor and was on the course to improve his musical skills in order to widen his scope in the theatre. He had a great sense of humour and even though I was permanently preoccupied, he managed to break through and put a silly smile on my face (where there had been a grimace, there was now a grinace).

I got through the week somehow and managed to write one or two passable numbers (not that passable is good enough in real life but not too bad in the circumstances). Sam was well aware of the pressure we were all under. Nevertheless, his standards were high so we did our very best

– and we all thought he was absolutely fabulous so how could we not give our all. My final meeting with Sam resulted in the interesting advice that I might think about writing a musical as my songs lent themselves quite well to that genre. Food for thought indeed. Overall, I wasn't sure just what I had achieved. I had been made aware that I didn't work well under that kind of pressure. I also had learned how close I was to having a nervous breakdown as I shouldn't have been that uptight the whole time. One or two of the others asked if they could tape a couple of my songs to take home with them. I was immensely flattered – unless they wanted to shore up their own fragile egos by playing my nondescript efforts. I'll never know.

We had a great last night. Polly surpassed herself with a terrific meal and then we all went down to the local pub. That in itself was quite an event as we hadn't been off the farm all week. Most of us were pretty pissed by now but the week had been one of comparative sobriety, so it was fair enough. The next morning we said our goodbyes, hugging each other in that strange way that people do after sharing an experience together; bonded for the moment so deeply that even one's nearest and dearest couldn't begin to understand. Five minutes later, you know the two you'll keep in touch with and the rest are already just a memory.

Annette dropped me off at the station. She was missing her family dreadfully and her relief to be on her way home was contagious. We promised to stay in touch (we have) and I waved her farewell. I cried all the way home. God knows why, my ordeal was over, yet I sobbed and sobbed. I was in a state. My life really was a mess. I look back now and I'm glad I went on the course. I did learn a lot from Sam but it was not the cathartic exercise I'd hoped it would be. And I was wrong to have gone thinking it would be the answer to all my problems.

I haven't attempted to write a musical yet but I have managed a couple of songs. Here are the lyrics to one I quite like:

# LIFE WAS BETTER THEN

## Verse 1

I've got a place in the middle of town
Lots of amusing people come round
We park our cars on yellow lines
Who cares about automobile fines
Who cares about anything very much

## Verse 2

When the going gets tough in the middle of town
We all light up and keep passing it round
And the world disappears in a cloud of smoke
And somebody tells a very bad joke
And we laugh like wayward children

## Chorus

But life was better then
Long ago when I was small
When I had nothing much at all
I had everything I could ever need.

## Verse 3

The bath stood by the kitchen mop
And doubled for a table top
The table was always cluttered though
With baking tins and carbolic soap
And I never remember having a bath

*The geraniums wept their orange tears*
*On the window sill throughout the years*
*And the window looked across the yard*
*Where iron railing stood on guard*
*I buy yellow roses these days*

*Repeat chorus*


My mother went mad when she heard it. "You didn't have a bath in the kitchen! What are you on about? People will think you're mad, writing stuff like that."

No, we didn't, but my grandmother (maternal!) did. She lived in Leeds. Beeston. Even the name is fairytale-ish (Grimms' admittedly). My mother had missed the whole point of the song. I wasn't having a go at dirty iron railings (although I did always go home after my weekly visits looking like a chimney sweep), or carbolic soap. I loved the carbolic soap – apart from the bits of wire wool that got embedded in the chunks.

It wasn't easy to write at home these days either, with all the building works around me – and I couldn't take my piano in the park. I soon slipped back into a slough of depression. Not difficult when four builders take up virtual residence in your bathroom for ten days.

# CHAPTER FIVE

I'd been putting off calling the plumber as I didn't fancy having a strange man around the place (well, maybe *in* the bath would be OK but not under it). But the leak had got so bad that even the carpet outside the bathroom door had begun to rot, so I reluctantly made the call to my landlords. I expected them to make the most of the situation – flood me out before finding the source – but never in my wildest dreams did I expect *four* men to turn up. It was only a leak in a bath, not the bloody Aswan Dam.

The men clumped through the front door, down my newly carpeted hall (laid after the last flood) and shuffled in servile fashion into the bathroom. The nightmare had begun.

"Cup of tea?" I asked after they'd settled in (five minutes), all signs of servility down the lavatory

"Wouldn't mind," they chorused.

"Strong, medium or weak?"

Feigning a degree of mateyness, I told the weak man that I couldn't drink dishwater, I liked mine strong. And then it just slipped out, "Like a navvy." *Please* let him be Scottish (Patrick O'Reilly *could* be). Later I wrote myself a memo on the back of my hand – 'don't mention the IRA or spuds.'

Over the next two weeks there was a lot of to-ing and fro-ing. It was too cold to leave the door open so I was jumping up and down every few minutes to let them back in with their wood and cement and whatever (the whole bathroom had to be ripped apart apparently, although I'll bet a new washer and a smidgeon of *Polyfilla* would have done the trick. The sheets they put down had more accumulated filth and debris on them than their clod-hopping footwear sported, so I wasn't impressed. In fact I preferred my own damp patch which in recent months had begun to resemble something I once saw in a modern art exhibition at the Tate gallery.

I had planned to catch up on begging letters to editors but my concentration followed their subservience down the plughole. I was on tenterhooks. Trapped in my living room, I felt like a rabbit caught in headlights – that is until the doorbell rang and I turned into Pavlov's dog. My main worry was that whilst I was hiding, one of the men would have an uncontrollable urge to wander behind the closed doors of my other rooms. Despite having sold everything of the remotest value, nevertheless I had still managed to create the illusion of modest grandeur (all the cracked items that were worthless looked good in subdued lighting). So I gave the impression of being worth a bob or two – also the porters had given out my résumé, therefore I must be rich if I'd been married to a pop star.

I'd taken the usual precautions of hiding personal documents in a safe place – unlike my mother who kept her 'grave' papers in the oven (no-one wants your grave, mother, believe me), as she always cooks on the rings only. However, one night she changed the habit of a lifetime and cooked roast pork garnished with cremated grave papers. I said it served her right and she wouldn't be able to die now.

Three of the men went off for a tea break (don't know what I'd been doing all morning), leaving one to hold the fort. 'Just go,' I silently pleaded, 'I can hold my own fort.' I asked him how long he thought the job would take. His reply of 'two or three weeks on and off' didn't register immediately as I noticed that his flies were undone. Our gazes interlocking, he pulled the zip up. Was it deliberate? Had his mates egged him on to do it and were they now talking dirty into their cracked mugs? Or was it an accident and was he mortified? No, he was not. I suspect it was a diversionary tactic to distract me from the 'two or three weeks on and off', when the landlords had said the job should only take a few days. It must have been that because I didn't even think about it until the next day. Well they could unzip their flies and take their stopcocks in and out to their hearts' content but *one* week was all they were going to get.

Various friends dropped in to lend support although on the whole, it was a pretty poor show. One arrived after the men had gone, two more cancelled, someone else rang to say their car had broken down ("Buy a new one, I'll pay for it – just get over here!"), another came with a heavy cold and sneezed all over me for two hours. Paul was more limp-wristed than usual, despite my warning that he wouldn't fancy anyone and what's more he might get *broken* wrists, never mind limp ones if he so much as glanced at a troublesome zip. Dominic was more of a nuisance than a help as he went into Frankie Howerd mode, thinking it would amuse the men. He was funny, I suppose, if you like that 'Ooh, Missus!' stuff – and he even looked like a younger version of him – but he was my solicitor and he was not being paid to entertain the enemy.

I rang an old friend, Rick, with a blow by blow account of how the building site mentality syndrome had been made flesh in my own flat.

"I wouldn't worry," he soothed. "We're not that bad."

I'd forgotten that Rick was a painter and decorator and winced at my insensitivity as he was probably the most courteous and well-mannered man I had ever met. Maybe my lot weren't so bad after all. I hadn't really given them a chance (and anyway, it was the landlords that my gripe was with). I would try to find a common meeting ground. We'd all sort out the country's problems (taxi drivers do not have the monopoly on this one). And there's snooker. I could suggest that we nip over to the Tap & Faucet after the next hard day on the job, for a game and a few dozen pints of Guinness. I used to drink Guinness all the time and before I moved south as a teenager, the 'in' drink was Tetley's Bitter. I also watch football on television – a legacy from an ex-boyfriend who put me on the same pedestal as his all-time hero, footballer Johann Cruyff. He would have volunteered to donate all his organs to him if needed, so I was flattered. Consequently, I've become a genuine football fan, although there isn't one I'd give *my* heart to. All in all, I really am 'one of the boys'. In fact I would probably make a damned good plumber.

Mission completed after a compromise of eight days, things quickly went back to normal – deep depression as against complete blackness of the soul. Actually, I don't think that I was clinically depressed so I shouldn't hijack that more serious description – which many of us invariably do through ignorance. I used to have a friend who was a psychiatrist at St. George's hospital before he went back to his native Australia. I often said I was depressed (and usually over the most trivial things) but Guy would correct me firmly, "You're unhappy L, not depressed." He had a real thing about people who hid behind clinical depression to justify what often amounted to whingeing and whining about their lot in life. When he had to listen to one of these so-called patients, he would nod thoughtfully – as doctors do, and appear to be making copious notes. And that would do the trick, give or take the odd placebo he might prescribe. In fact, the notes he wrote were more often than not to his friends. I received one such letter complaining that he was "listening to this woman moaning about the trivial problems in her life and I want to scream at her, 'We've all got crap to put up with, you stupid, boring cretin, just fuck off and stop wasting my time when there are people out there with *real* problems.' But obviously I can't. Anyway, thanks for listening L, I feel much better now."

Even psychiatrists need someone to talk to as the pressure is enormous. Guy would therefore sometimes ring me late at night to offload – although he never mentioned who his patients were except on one occasion when he let Princess Margaret's name slip out. He covered his mistake quickly, though, so I was never sure what the inference was. I became a voice of reason, particularly where his own personal life was concerned.

Guy had a live-in boyfriend and the relationship was

very volatile, so a good old chin-wag about our love-lives was most cathartic. He was great fun and I would often go to his flat in Battersea for dinner – he was a good cook – and we would curl up in bed together afterwards and watch old movies. His boyfriend, Les, would waft around in the other room as he wasn't into Joan Crawford or Bette Davies. "I live with a bitch. I don't need to watch them as well."

Once when my mother came to stay, Guy popped over for Sunday lunch as Les had gone away for a few days. Like the rest of us (apart from my mother who only had a vat of sweet sherry at Christmas, although she would insist that she only had a 'thimbleful'), Guy got very drunk and it was only later that we realised he was missing. My mother went to look for him and a moment or two later came back, laughing nervously.

"Lily, love, he's in your bed. And he's taken his clothes off. Ooh, I don't know, a psychiatrist as well! None of my friends will believe it." Respect for the medical profession was so ingrained in my mother and her generation that it was anathema to catch one of them with his trousers down.

Guy was quite possessive and liked to keep me all to himself but tolerated my various affairs and flings as he saw them for what they were – long before I did, naturally – and so meeting Graham presented no problem. I had told him that I'd finally found the person I wanted to spend the rest of my life with and I wanted him and Les to come over for dinner and meet him. I really meant it this time but, as I always said that, Guy had no reason to believe that Graham was any different from all the others.

I had met Graham Sewell at a recent party. He was with a rowdy group of blokes but we kept exchanging meaningful looks, as I knew he wasn't like the rest. Wrong. Of course he was (he even shared a house with five of them), but he was the most gorgeous chap I'd ever seen. Strange, because looks don't particularly interest me (James Woods?) – and my daughters can testify to that – but his face was so beautiful that I couldn't take my eyes off him. He came over eventually and we flirted wildly. He was very, very funny, too. So, looks *and* humour, a deadly combination. He said that he was in 'educational books'. Looks, humour, intelligence, I'd hit the jackpot. The only slight drawback was his age. I do keep falling for younger men, but it is definitely not a sex thing, it's the juvenile humour that appeals to me. Mind you, Graham was very sexy as well. And when Guy set eyes on him he not only saw the attraction but he also knew instinctively that this was the big one. So what did he do?

He spent the entire evening with his back to Graham, ignoring him whenever he tried to engage him in conversation – or humming rather than answering. He bitched away with Les about tulips and clogs, something like that, as he knew that Graham was half-Dutch. As soon as the embarrassing meal was over, he helped me wash up, at my behest, and quickly said how nice Graham was and how he could tell that he was 'the one'. So why was he behaving so badly and trying to ensure that Graham would never want to see me again? He denied it but I was beside myself with rage and told him to leave with Les immediately and never, ever contact me again. And when he did ring some time later in the hope that things had calmed down, I reiterated my feelings on the matter and then he got the message. It was over. However, Graham and I went on to live happily ever after together. For the next two years, that is.

# CHAPTER SIX

Money was becoming a real concern as I wasn't earning enough to pay my bills now. I hated signing on as it was such a problem, particularly being self-employed. Because my earnings fluctuated slightly each week I had to fill in forms, produce proof of earnings and provide numerous other documents on a regular basis (often fortnightly) and then wait for it to be assessed before I got benefit (Jobseekers Allowance/Income Support), so it was easier eventually *not* to claim my rights. I *was* receiving housing benefit, otherwise I couldn't have paid my rent.

I loathed being on benefit and desperately wanted to come off it as soon as possible. Dominic was supportive, which kept me just this side of sane, but he was also beginning to behave slightly oddly. I invited him to some friends to dinner, assuming he'd be on top form. After the introductions he thanked Elizabeth for the glass of wine and until he thanked her for dinner and said goodbye, he never spoke another word. He stared at his feet and his plate for the whole evening, so he was unaware of my black looks (and I couldn't kick him because he was just out of reach). It was so weird that the other guests were openly asking, 'Is he alright?' I said if he were, he wouldn't be later. Elizabeth and Ben were very kind and said it didn't matter at all, as there was obviously a problem. Although I noticed he didn't have a problem clearing his plate, so it wasn't his stomach. It was just the most bizarre behaviour. We left early (surprise) and I berated him all the way home. Still he didn't say anything. He even came into my flat and let me carry on for another couple of hours, neither offering an explanation nor putting up a defence. I never really found out what had happened that night.

"I just go quiet like that sometimes" was all he would say.

At least I had Kieran to fall back on as he'd come back into my life now that I had split with Dan. He too was very amusing although, like many 'clowns', he never knew when to stop. I always had to push him out of the door when I was tired of his incessant banter. He was always trying to cheer me up as I was 'boring and too miserable by half'. Probably because men wouldn't be taken advantage of in the same way as women in my situation are (the landlords would never have attempted the suspected harassment if I'd had a partner living with me). It was difficult for them to fully appreciate how it could give one a sense of humour bypass. Also, being so obsessed with everything that was going on, I was naturally distracted and wasn't laughing at his jokes as much as he would have liked.

I first met Kieran in 1982 at Camden Palace. I'd gone there with a friend. We'd been out a few times, nothing serious, but we'd always had a good time. However, that particular night he made a beeline for admittedly rather a gorgeous girl and spent the evening hanging on to her every word (it was later proved love at first sight as they eventually did get married). I was disgruntled, understandably, but there were other people I knew so I didn't mind too much. A tall, attractive fellow with long hair, wearing a ballet-style shirt and stretch black jeans was watching me. He eventually came over and said, "As your man has left you, I thought I'd keep you company, please. She's pretty, but not as pretty as you. She is wearing very nice hairspray though. Do you want to go for a kebab?"

I laughed at his nonsense, but declined. "No thanks, I don't know you."

"Damn. I didn't bring my birth certificate. I have a receipt for the dry cleaners," he said, fishing one out of his pocket.

"It's not your name I want proof of. Have you got a character reference?" I was beginning to warm to the game.

"I have. In Wales."

"Is that where you're from?"

"I live in Muswell Hill. My parents and a few cars are in Wales."

"Are you a second hand car salesman?"

"I'm a second hand car *buyer*."

It appeared that he bought classic cars and did them up for pleasure, occasionally selling the odd one when he ran out of parking spaces. At any one time he could have as many as twenty. For a living he bought run-down property, did the places up (rewiring, plumbing, painting and decorating – the works) and sold them on.

We started going out together although I knew that he was also involved with someone else. He was very secretive about her, which didn't bother me at first but it would eventually. He would forgetfully double-book and I was the one he cancelled because Carole didn't know about me. And there was the time he arranged to come for a New Year's dinner with me and my family, but he had also arranged to go to Carole's for the same thing. He popped in, saying he'd have the starter with us as he couldn't let her down 'and she doesn't do starters.' I said if he didn't stay for the whole meal I'd taken two days to prepare (those bloody starters the least of the culinary effort), then I'd never see him again. So he wolfed the whole lot down before going on to have another blow-out (minus the starter) with Carole. I rather hoped she concentrated on suet puddings and thick custard.

He often came to stay the night and in those days Aids was something only gay men caught. How ignorant was that. The reality, of course, was different but the facts hadn't surfaced properly in those hedonistic days. So getting pregnant was the main problem, give or take catching an anti-social disease – and a course of penicillin would sort that out quickly – therefore condoms were a thing of the past. The only time I would worry was when Kieran said, "I've got your coil stuck on my leg." I fell for it every time. I still only had his dry cleaning ticket for a reference, so I should have been more careful (and I didn't know who else Carole was sleeping with), but I wasn't. And of course, neither was he.

I hated it when he came round still covered in brick dust as he didn't like having baths over much. I used to say that I was going to have a bath to get rid of the brick dust that had seeped in from the building site, hoping that he would take the hint and want to get rid of his own, but the nearest he got was to come in the bathroom to see how well I was scrubbing up and say, "It's a pity to waste the bath water, perhaps I'll take it home with me in a plastic bag." He never did much with his hair either – or so he pretended for a laugh, "I'll leave washing my hair for another week, then I'll just have to poke it with a stick."

When he got done for speeding or perhaps something more serious - I can't remember exactly – anyway he had to go to court so it probably was something very serious, he was fussing about what to wear.

"Don't even think ballet shirt and skin tight jeans, you have to wear a suit," I told him.

"Will that get me off?"

"It will help, perhaps."

"Then I'll wear two suits, that should do the trick."

I only went to music related events with Kieran as I once made the mistake of taking him to see an actor friend in Shakespeare's *Pericles*. Unfortunately, we were on the very front row and Brian could see us. Kieran was giggling and whispering throughout. At one point Brian came in with a crown that did admittedly resemble a bowl with asparagus stalks round it, so naturally Kieran wanted to know why Brian had a dip on his head. I was absolutely mortified when he said in a whisper that put the stage prompts to shame, "I'd better get some sleep now." How could Brian be anything but furious with us. I knew that I was now off his Christmas card list. But the worst was yet to come. A good twenty minutes before the curtain, Kieran said – and I truly think his 'whisper' was so loud that even the upper circle heard him, "Dost thou think we can goest now?"

Music industry do's were another matter. Keen rock fans, Kieran and I were regular pairings at most of them. When an invitation arrived for me he would look at the name on the envelope, mine naturally, and would say sadly, "They've spelt my name entirely wrong again."

There was no doubt that I was entertained but I paid for it in kind. As well as the parties, I gave lavish dinners at home (I had money to entertain in those days), to which Kieran was frequently invited. One particular night, there was a more eclectic group of people in contrast to the usual music-orientated people I tended to mix with. Kieran looked at the name cards (I did things in style, too) and was horrified. "I will only be able to talk to Val about the chair I've made out of Fairy Liquid bottles and, as I don't know the other people, perhaps you could make me a little place *under* the table."

His parents had a farm in Wales (sheep and old Buicks.) He went to public school, which probably accounted for many things, especially the way he raided my fridge and consumed the contents there and then, shovelling them into his face like there was no tomorrow. I never met his father, but his mother was a delight. Kieran clearly thought the world of her but I wished he wouldn't tell her about his bedroom habits as I felt embarrassed when I had to speak to her. She took it all in her stride apparently. He had been married once and had remained on close terms with his ex-wife. She sounded lovely – a tolerant and understanding person – but I'll bet even her patience was stretched when it came to fridges.

I hadn't seen Kieran since I'd been married to Dan, as Dan naturally wasn't keen on having ex-boyfriends around the place, so it was reassuring to find that he hadn't changed. He hadn't changed at all in fact as the trousers were still the same, although looking now more Spinal Tap than Rock God. He still was physically very attractive and still had his great sense of humour. But he also continued to raid my fridge, which these days often yielded nothing more than a meagre portion of cottage cheese and cheap plonk, so I wouldn't be too pleased when my dinner disappeared. That apart, he was a tonic at times. He did get fed up with my dark moods but rather than leave me to them he would then try to give me pep talks in the hope that I would 'snap out' of my misery.

I thought his pep talks were crap as they frequently resulted in making me feel that everything was my fault (how I could be responsible for the running of the social services and the mindsets of avaricious landlords was a mystery). So we did have quite a few rows but he never bore grudges and after wisely leaving me to cool off for a couple of weeks or so, he would be back at my door as daft and hungry as ever.

# CHAPTER SEVEN

Depressed, unhappy, whatever the diagnosis, things were not good. I was beginning to feel disconnected from reality, as though I were hovering a foot or so above the ground whilst everyone else was firmly rooted. I wasn't sleeping properly and when I did drop off, my 'bus' dreams came thick and fast. I'd been dreaming about buses for years (even when I was normal) and they were more or less always the same. I would be in a strange town (although eventually the town would become familiar as I dreamt about it so often), and it was imperative that I caught a bus although my destination was always hazy. I was never at the right stop, however, and had to run wildly to the next one which was often a mile or so away. When I did catch one, getting on was never easy as I was usually carrying an awkward piece of furniture, which the driver would make me leave in a nearby shop to collect later. Or I would have to haul myself up the back of the bus to get on, through an upstairs window. I know life is a journey, but this was ridiculous. I just don't know why I couldn't get a tube occasionally for a change.

I went to see my doctor although I knew he wouldn't be able to help with my nocturnal travel arrangements, but at least I hoped he would make a willing and reliable witness should I ever have to go to court over the landlords. He listened sympathetically and even gave me a dolly mixture out of the ever-present jar on his desk, reserved normally for children.

"I can't give you what you need. I wish I could," he finally said.

"And what's that?"

"Money."

"Money?" I echoed.

"Yes. You need to get away from your landlords as that's where all your problems lie, I believe. It's obviously all very stressful for you – all the symptoms sound very stress-related to me."

I asked him if he would put it in writing should I need him to and he said he would be glad to. Meanwhile, he suggested that I saw one of his counsellors as she might be able to help.

Yes!! I was nearly officially depressed! I felt the pavement beneath my feet for once, when I left the surgery.

My appointment with the counsellor fell on a Tuesday, the day I was scheduled to share a stand with Emma at one of the quarterly fairs I did at Sandown Park Racecourse. I hadn't realised until the night before, so I couldn't change the appointment. It was a shame though, because even if I only made a few pounds, I might at least have got rid of some old stock which I was sick and tired of seeing (as, it would appear, was everyone else). In fact, I sold something recently that I'd had for seven years. It had originally cost me forty-five pounds but I was more than happy to let it go for eighteen.

The assumption that all antiques, if kept long enough automatically increase in value, is a fallacy. Like the fickle fashion world, there are fads and trends which dictate the market. At the top end the risk is obviously greater, as thousands of pounds can be tied up in an item past its sell-by date. The average dealer who hasn't thousands to invest in a single piece spreads the risk, but inevitably, often gets caught out. It's interesting how something that was once aesthetically pleasing, due in part to its age, can become quite ugly *because* of its age – the dust of time being one thing, shelf dust something else.

Moving things around helps and an item can sell simply because in a different position it looks like a new acquisition (and cleaned, a totally different object). Indeed, an eye-catching new juxtaposition worked recently when I sold a brooch dramatically displayed on a green-silk-lined box to a dealer who must have seen it every week for the past two years. Then again, maybe not, as it was a jet brooch and had been in a black box.

When I go into a shop, I hate not being able to see the prices, as something marked 'ten shillings' does give one a rough idea of how long the dealer has had it. I confess though that I hide the price stickers as I think they're ugly and spoil the symmetry, but then I'm not guilty of the hard sell like some dealers are. If someone asks me the price of an item I will not inform then that it's 'beautiful' unless they have a white stick and I will not state the obvious and say, for example, that it's made of glass unless I'm sure that the customer is either under five, senile or ham-handed. Its history only interests the customer if the price is right, so a voluntary lecture – often inaccurate – is unwelcome. I rarely stay for this as by then I'm ready to dash this now undesirable item to the floor. I almost prefer the attitude of the dealer I overheard this week when asked by his wife if something they had was English. "It doesn't matter, it's twenty pounds – right?"

There are dealers who don't mind having stickers because everything is in code. Not even a MENSA member could crack some of them (if A=10, etc.) – unless twenty two thousand pounds *is* the current price for a dented cigarette case? I don't know, I haven't bought one recently. Codes are meant to deter the 'We have one of those, I wonder what it's worth?' brigade. This does work but only when people have had their teeth clamped, otherwise most people usually find that saying 'How much?' does the trick.

Another thing that puts me off buying is when a shop is absolutely crammed from floor to ceiling. It makes me feel physically tired. Where does one begin? And do I need to worry about knocking things off their precarious perches, breaking them and having to buy the bits? This happened in reverse at the last Sandown Park fair. I was looking after a friend's stall for a few minutes and an American, middle-aged woman – obviously not a dealer – picked up an Art Nouveau decanter and, without holding the stopper, turned it upside down (a dealer would never have been so careless) and naturally, the stopper fell out and crashed onto the matching glasses. It was a pretty stupid thing to do anyway and when she saw the price of the set - £250, she was mortified. I really wasn't sure what to do as one of the glasses was now chipped, spoiling an otherwise perfect set.

"I'll come back and see the young man," she volunteered. But how could I be certain that she would? Seeing my hesitation, she opened her purse and pushed £50 into my hand, again apologised profusely, and left. When Gerald returned he was not too put out as the glass could be ground down. So with the compensation money, he bought a very nice bottle of wine ( from a friend who put his Paris antique-buying trips to good use with a lucrative little side-line) which we drank out of two of the remaining undamaged glasses – after we'd wiped the shelf dust off, of course.

The counsellor was much younger than I had expected, in her thirties possibly, and very attractive. I liked her immediately and felt instantly at ease. She said I should call her Linda, another reason why I felt relaxed about baring my soul to a stranger. She had my doctor's report but wanted to hear my account so I filled her in as quickly as possible, as I thought it otherwise too self-indulgent to give her a blow-by-blow picture (and the session was only for an hour, not six months). Also I was worried that she might start writing to her friends if I droned on about Kanga drills and seventies flares for too long.

Inevitably, she wanted to hear about my childhood. Talking about one's problems is one thing but a monologue about one's background is another. It somehow seems impolite. I was brought up to show interest in the other party and not hog the limelight. So I wanted to draw her in, ask her where *she* was born, who *her* friends were, etc., but of course it was not that sort of situation. Again, I tried to be as brief as possible – also I wasn't convinced that my past had anything to do with my present predicament.

I had a conventional background. My father was a fireman, my mother a happy housewife. We lived in Bradford, in Yorkshire. I was an only child (did I see Linda perk up at this giveaway?) I had loads of friends (sorry Linda, back to the drawing board) and I went to the Ritz cinema every Saturday morning. Sunday was chapel day, Sunday school *and* evening service. I hated the afternoon session but I couldn't wait to go again in the evening as I'd fallen in love with one of the regulars, Malcolm Jones. I was thirteen and he was fifteen. I stayed faithful to him for four years despite the fact that he never once asked me out. I learned years later that he couldn't stand my bitten nails. And to think that I used to pray to God all the way home from chapel every Sunday, 'Please let me go out with Malcolm Jones.' He could have dropped hints about the nails. I went off God after that. A sort of road to Damascus moment in reverse, only in my case it was the road to Eastbrook Hall chapel.

I sang in talent contests which I sometimes won but I felt stupid and so I eventually rebelled. I once went to Butlins holiday camp at Filey with my parents when I was six and my mother made me enter a beauty contest. I cried all the way through it and looked more like a candidate for the ugly bug ball. I came last.

I was brainy, apparently, and as an infant I was paraded around the more senior classes at school and made to demonstrate my reading skills. Oddly, I was given the *Yorkshire Post* to read aloud from – although why a bunch of six-year olds would want to know about the share index going down and oil prices going up, I'll never fathom. I later went to the second-best grammar school (already my brains were in decline) where, according to my over-devoted mother, I 'got in with the wrong crowd', neatly justifying my miserable academic record.

My parents clearly adored me, my mother to the point of madness. I was obviously the most talented and gorgeous child who ever lived, so it was always a mystery when I was sent to bed for a misdemeanour I'd committed. And my weekly pocket money was nothing to shout about.

We moved houses in the Bradford area every two or three years as it was my mother's hobby. We only deviated once when we went to live in Arnside, a small estuary village in the Lake District. I was eight. My father had left the fire service by this time as my mother couldn't tolerate the shift work any longer. He had risen to Section Officer and his workload was heavy. My father loved his job but he loved my mother more, so with heavy heart (concealed from her but not escaping my notice, despite my tender years), he took a job as an estate manager.

We lived in a Gothic-style stone lodge at the entrance to the grounds of the house. There were owls and red squirrels in our garden, as the woods of the estate adjoined. Even though the water's edge and soft grassy dunes were only a stone's throw from our front door, I preferred the long climb up Arnside Knott – a hilly protuberance with magnificent views over Arnside, the surrounding countryside and Morecambe Bay in the distance. There were ancient trees (two, I'm sure, were fossilised giraffes locked together, not trees) and natural ready-made dens to add my own DIY touches to. I was never afraid to be there on my own despite being so young – one's parents were not on red alert as they are today. The murder of a child was virtually unheard of. However, perhaps if my mother had known that Ripper-in-waiting, teenager Peter Sutcliffe was perhaps also hiding in the dens on the Knott, she might have exercised more caution (he apparently stayed in nearby Silverdale in the summer holidays). As it was, I once got lost up there and I did get quite scared – only that I would be late home for tea. Luckily, a man on a bicycle came by and said that he would show me the way but first of all he would take me back to his house and his wife would give me some eggs (I might not have gone with him if he'd said 'sweets' as I'd heard about men who gave children sweets, they made them go and work down coal mines and never see their mummies or daddies again). But he said eggs. And eggs were what I got. In a blue bag. As I said earlier, I've led a charmed life.

My father always lost money when we sold houses as he wasn't a business man, but if it made my mother happy then he was happy. Their needs were simple as they didn't drink or go out on the town (my father smoked ten *Woodbines* a day, which was his only luxury) and anyway, they had a wide circle of friends so their lives were full. If money did become a problem we would take in the odd lodger. We had a couple of acrobats from Chipperfields Circus once, which was great because they taught me how to somersault. Not so great was the time my primary school teacher came to stay. I never liked him after he deliberately dropped one of the rock cakes that my mother had let me have a go at making. It broke the plate. My mother said it was an accident. It wasn't. He had deliberately held it on a level with his spotty forehead and then dropped it. My mother changed her mind, however, a few weeks later when she found pornographic pictures of his girlfriend under his bed. So she asked him to leave. I think the girlfriend would have done too if she'd known because only the head was hers, the naked bodies were all different, cut from various magazines.

Our longest boarder, Bhim Tamang, was from Darjeeling. My father loved his company and would sit late into the night discussing anything and everything with him. My mother even learnt how to make Bhim's favourite curries (which was amazing as she wasn't noted for her culinary skills – I have known her to 'put the carrots on' when I was leaving Kings Cross, in readiness for my arrival three hours later).

I was Bhim's 'little sister' and we used to flick through the Bollywood-style film magazines together as he loved my reactions to some of the unfamiliar names – like Ashit. That one got me every time. I learnt that when Sir Edmund Hillary and Tenzing Norgay conquered Everest, Bhim was invited to play host and interpreter to Tenzing on his lap of honour around London.

He went but refused to be photographed standing next to him as he said that his father would disown him if he saw the photos because the Tamangs were from a high caste Gurkha background, whilst the mighty Tenzing was from a low caste Sherpa one. I thought Bhim was a terrible snob and I wouldn't speak to him for weeks after I heard about this but as I was a juvenile delinquent (according to him) and ignorant of others' customs and religions, what did I know. So I said in that case I'd stop having him for a brother, as a mixed race family just wasn't the custom in our street. Eventually we made up, smoked the pipe of peace – sorry, wrong Indians – chewed a couple of betel nuts and went to the pictures. However, for a long time afterwards I did call him by a new name. Ashit.

Controversy as to who actually reached the summit first still rages today. Was it Sir Edmund Hillary? Or was it Tenzing Norgay? According to Bhim it was Tenzing. Apocryphal? Fellow-countryman's patriotism? Or perhaps just maybe. Who will ever know now? Apparently Tenzing's family don't know to this day. Perhaps it's for the best as it was a joint feat of superhuman endeavour and as such, both maybe deserve equal credit.

I took piano lessons for three years but as I only practised the night before I had the lesson, I could only play basic tunes. My mother had been the school pianist as a girl, which meant that her education suffered as a result. She liked playing hymns – but never at their normal speed as she loved a good sing. So *The Old Rugged Cross* would end up sounding like Vera Lynn on speed. Her favourite was *Surely Goodness and Mercy*. She didn't so much play as syncopate (make amendments). She loved her hymns so much that we had a full-sized organ installed in our humble thirties pebble-dash semi . The pipes had to be sawn in half to get it in the front room. The odd thing is that no-one complained about the noise. Perhaps the neighbours thought we were a small Pentecostal church.

I, too, liked singing now. I joined a Yorkshire Jazz Band when I was sixteen as vocalist in residence. We played mainly in and around Yorkshire but occasionally we ventured further afield and one night we were booked into the Cavern in

Liverpool. We'd already done a gig earlier in the evening in Manchester, so it was a bit of a dash. I had drunk half a bottle of rum by the time we arrived and my first number was therefore prophetic – *Nobody knows You When You're Down And Out*. The trombonist could be heard muttering, "get her off" (I don't think it was 'Get *'em* off'). I thoroughly enjoyed myself, however, and got through another number, *St James' Infirmary Blues* (where I rightly should have been), before I was discreetly propelled off the stage.

I left home at eighteen, never to return.

A perfectly ordinary childhood, then. Nothing for Linda to get her teeth into there.

# CHAPTER EIGHT

Recently my flat had been plunged into total darkness as scaffolding had gone up outside. However, it wasn't simply metal bars and wooden planks I had for a view now, but also a vast hoist to carry materials and debris up and down to the penthouses that were being built. For the best part of nine months, I would have to contend with the cranking and clanging of this monstrous blight on my daily life. I couldn't open most of my windows, as the struts were right up to them. The filth and rubble continued to pile up to my sills, as the rubbish collector couldn't get along the blocked channel to clear it. I once attempted to squeeze my way through as I was worried that rats might have taken up residence, but I almost fell down a manhole that had carelessly been left open. Ladders were often left propped up, tempting would-be burglars (the scaffolding around my flat was not alarmed, only the upper floors were given protection). One night a man climbed down one of the ladders. Again my mother was with me and she shouted at him. This brought the head porter out with a flashlight and the chap legged it before anyone could catch him.

I dreaded opening the post, as hardly a day went by without there being something horrible to contend with. The DSS was indeed one of the main culprits, but the landlords were in a class of their own. Not that they always wrote to tell me when major works in my vicinity would be starting – that would be for me to discover. But often some officious letter would arrive, usually planned for a Saturday morning, when I would be unable to contact anyone about it, thus ensuring that I would have a miserable and apprehensive weekend. One such intimidating missive arrived, putting the telephone reminder and excessive water rates in the shade. Dangerous asbestos was to be removed from the basement area and, as my flat was part of it, I would have to vacate it whilst this remedial work was carried out. Now, I was aware that at that time, in the early nineties, the government had advised that both blue and brown asbestos should be removed, as they *were* dangerous. Schools and hospitals in particular were very vulnerable. There was indeed asbestos here and there in the basement area, and the pipes in the false ceiling of my hall were lagged with a mixture of asbestos and something else. It was white asbestos which I'd heard was safe to live with, providing it wasn't badly damaged. I said that I wouldn't move out as that was the one thing that Dominic and other lawyers had stressed - particularly if it necessitated moving out with all my furniture – as once I'd gone, ostensibly for a short period, I could be barred from getting back in for years, on some pretext or another. Meanwhile, work to remove the pipes in the corridor outside of my door had begun, but as the area was scheduled for redevelopment eventually (once I'd gone), then the old pipes would have been pulled out anyway.

I had to walk through plastic tunnels to get in and out through my front door for two or three weeks, no doubt inhaling some pretty unpleasant dust, asbestos or otherwise. The landlords' solicitors waffled about health and safety, their rights etc., and wanted my assurance by return that I would let the men in the moon suits in a.s.a.p. I rang Westminster Council asbestos wing and explained my situation to a nice sounding chap. He said he would come and inspect. He did a thorough check and told me what I had suspected all along, that there was no danger from the pipe lagging. At my request he wrote a back-up letter and I presented it to the landlords' solicitors. (I could have sent it straight to the landlords, but I knew they would have to pay, so I am told, something like £100 to hear it from their lawyers).

I never heard about the lethal asbestos again.

A producer I'd worked with in the past was now at Talk Radio and so I got regular work for a few months on his show, a music orientated programme which only bit the dust because Talk went sport mad and didn't want anything more exciting than rain to interrupt play.

The first person I suggested interviewing was Kevin Godley as I'd heard that he was in the final stages of editing a video or rather *fifteen* into one, for the forthcoming Comic Relief BBC TV extravaganza. I've interviewed him before, both as producer and musician and enjoyed his company, as he's sharp and funny so I knew I was in for a good time. I was intrigued to find out how he pulled off such a mammoth undertaking (fifteen artistes all with their separate story boards).

"What was amazing about it which I've never experienced before in a shoot, people were arriving 'cos they had a little window in their day – it was like Casualty, people were backing up like waiting for beds. Say Mel Smith between two and three. Right, it's two fifteen, get him in, let's do something. Get him out. Right, we've got Mystic Meg. In with Mystic Meg. Out with Mystic Meg. It was crazy.

"I think the hit of the shoot – and I use the word literally – was Jane Couch (the boxer). She was only in one shot, she was hot, man. She came out there and she was really hyped up. She didn't want to hit a rubber ball, she wanted to hit people. And she hit *me*. She did, like WALLOP! Right on the side of my face. I think she pulled a punch at the last minute. Then she chased the AD around the studio and beat the crap out of him."

"What was she on?" I asked, sensing a solution to my next encounter with the landlords.

Disappointingly Kevin replied, "Nothing. Just adrenalin. That was an extraordinary moment. My jaw still clicks." He then cried out in mock indignation, "I may sue. Listen." He wiggled his jaw about and I swear it sounded like the percussive backing to *Agadoo*. I'd definitely sue.

Kevin laughed good-naturedly, "At the end of the day it worked because each person that came in brought something to it. It was fun to do and hopefully it will help raise a lot of money for a great cause." And needless to say, it did.

Now it's an accepted fact that unless you are a complete anorak, you do not accost well known personalities when they are 'off duty' - that is eating in restaurants or shopping with their hair in curlers – so I usually go through agents or personal contacts to arrange an interview. However, agents can be very protective of their clients so it's not always possible to talk to the people one would like to. Therefore when an opportunity arises, it is very tempting to take advantage of the situation. As I live in the centre of London, I frequently bump into famous people unencumbered by zealous agents or sycophantic minders, indeed often looking quite approachable. There are of course the ones that even a deranged fan would give a wide berth to. There was Ken Russell, for example, looking extremely hot and bothered bearing down on me at 80 mph – better not stop him in his tracks or he might spontaneously combust. Or Jimmy Young, marching determinedly in the direction of the BBC with the single mindedness of a man with only five minutes to On-Air, would not be amused by my opening line, "Excuse me, Mr. Young, could I just have a couple of minutes of your time…" Then there was Richard E. Grant studiously avoiding eye contact in a busy street, although he need not have bothered as no one was looking at him, but rather his gorgeous daughter. I wondered whether to ask her if she collected anything (I was writing at the time on celebrities who collect antiques) but as she was bawling her head off, I decided not to bother.

Nothing compares, though, to the time Bob Geldof – a regular interviewee of mine, good chap – asked me to introduce him to Prince, as he was then known. I'd interviewed Prince earlier in the day through his manager, as he wasn't talking. I'd just assumed that he hated the press and would rather meet fellow musicians. We were at the Embassy Club in London's Bond Street, a popular hangout for both musicians and annoying people with microphones at the ready (come on, I'll bet surgeons carry tiny scalpels around with them?), so it should have been OK to stroll over to the diminutive fellow tucked away in a dark corner and introduce Sir Bob-to-be. I reminded him of our earlier non-speaking conversation and then said Bob would like to meet him also. He promptly hid behind his manager, leaving Bob to say how much he liked his records and how he admired him (the manager looked bemused). Bob made several attempts to catch his eye but he was having none of it and in the end Bob slunk away muttering, "That was the most embarrassing moment of my life." For ages afterwards I thought Prince had an affliction which meant he could sing but not talk.

There he was at the toothpaste counter, the lovely Michael Palin. I apologised and explained why I'd come between him and a tube of minty freshener. He flashed me a smile so dazzling that I bought six tubes of the stuff afterwards.

"I don't collect anything, I'm afraid. I've brought all sorts of bits and pieces back from my travels but there's nothing you could say was the basis for a collection. I'm so sorry."

So was I. Still, I'd crossed the barrier of good taste and it wasn't that bad being an anorak – not when the object of one's desire was so charming. I could probably now stroll up to Al Pacino in a restaurant, his mouth full of French fries, and discuss antiques until the cheese board came. Or until he smacked me in the face.

Barbara Windsor chatted happily in the local grocery store, no make-up, her hair in curlers – I swear, go on, ring her up. Ask her (she did wear a little nylon scarf to hide them). How many actresses with a glamorous image would let themselves be seen out like that? I thought she was great. Mind you, it's always the way when you dash out without your eyes or lipstick on and wearing a ragbag assortment of charity shop rejects, you're bound to bump into someone you know. Or want to know.

On one such occasion I went shopping to Soho's Berwick Street market and looked up to see Terence Stamp talking amicably to a stallholder. TERENCE STAMP! I might just have time to dash home, put on my lipliner,

Armani suit and new pink Doc Martens. Or was he more of a stiletto man? I could *not* let him see me looking like I did. But I couldn't let him go either. There was nothing for it but to feebly rearrange my fringe (well, you never know) and boldly step forward. Our eyes met across the broccoli. He looked amused, I thought. I expect he sensed my dilemma. In between buying two pounds of onions, he told me that he collected Rupert Bear annuals. We bade farewell and I swear that for a moment, he didn't think I looked that bad. Then I caught sight of myself in a mirror. A cheap mirror though, not a true reflection.

I did once get as far as tagging along with Cliff Richard as he was leaving a tennis court. "I'm sorry to bother you," I began. "You're not," he replied cheerfully and marched off. Ouch.

I was compiling a feature for Talk on the sixties and I decided to give Shadows guitarist and vocalist, Bruce Welch, a call as I'd recently met him at a party. He'd entertained everyone long into the small hours playing a medley of his songs (he has also written numerous hits for other artistes). There were other songwriters there, but even they only wanted to 'singalongaBruce'.

He was more than happy to do the interview and we made arrangements for him to come to the flat one lunchtime. I knew the workmen knocked off for lunch between 12.30 and 1.30 so I reckoned that we had possibly thirty, even forty-five minutes. I would have to edit the tape to twenty minutes anyway, so any longer would be pointless. That's the thing about working in radio, so much is edited out as time is of the essence. A lot had to be crammed into the couple of hours; it was rare to devote this magazine style programme to one single person, however famous.

I had spoken to the head porter earlier to make doubly certain that he would delay the workmen should they get drill withdrawal symptoms and decide to come back early. A bit of a Shadows fan in his youth, he was willing to help. Unfortunately, he didn't reckon with the new team that had moved into a storeroom adjacent to my flat at precisely the moment when the others knocked off. So the drills outside had stopped but now not only were drills in action a few feet away, but also stone floors were being smashed with sledgehammers. Bruce had arrived a few minutes before, so we were taken completely unawares. We both jumped out of our skins when it started up – no one of course had bothered to tell me that major works were to take place on my doorstep. I had only just nicely got rid of the plastic tunnels, and now this.

I rang the porter's office but my go-between was equally in the dark, as he was only fed information that the landlords wanted him to know (or impart). I realised that he was in an awkward position, as he had to keep peace with the residents and at the same time maintain his relationship with his employers. Therefore I was aware that there was nothing he could do about it. So I 'sandbagged' the doors as best I could and found the quietest corner in the flat to do the interview. Bruce luckily had a sense of humour as we had to sit hunched in a bit of the hall, switching the UHER off when it got too noisy and then re-doing the section again when the men stopped for a quick game of footie with a lump of concrete.

Unfortunately, the interview subsequently had to be cut to just four minutes as the drills were more or less there the whole time in the background and could not be eliminated. However, Kelly liked those few minutes enough to invite Bruce to the studio in the near future and have the whole programme more or less to himself. (As I mentioned previously, this was most unusual). Bruce would get to sing and play as well so, inadvertently, the drills did him a favour. I, on the other hand, couldn't risk interviewing anyone else at my flat now. I'd never had problems getting people to drop in, as it was so central, but I would now have to make different arrangements. Talk didn't pay expenses, so I only hoped I wouldn't have to interview someone in Scotland, as Vauxhall was my limit on foot.

Meanwhile, back at the RANCH (Rubble Aggravation

Noise Constant Headache), the ferocious banging was making my flat vibrate. In the nearest room, pictures were actually dislodged. I live in a part of the basement that was not originally designated for anything other than storerooms, so my area, the largest of the interlocking rooms, wasn't turned into a flat until the late sixties, when I moved in. But now it looked as though the two cupboard-sized rooms next to me were about to be turned into something habitable. I gathered later that one of the management company officials might use it as his office (he wouldn't be getting any cups of sugar from me, that's for sure). I also found out that the workmen (who would become my close neighbours on and off for the next eighteen months) were being deployed from the flats they were working on in other parts of the building. Their instructions, it would appear, were to bash away at walls and drill for a couple of hours on an ad hoc basis, so that I never knew when the noise was going to start (or stop). As the walls kept going up and coming down again, I began to wonder if this was all part of a 'creative harassment' plan.

The workmen would leave the door open of the room they were working in so that not only was the noise far greater, but also the corridor was filled with clouds of cement and brick dust. As I was now officially living in a building site and needed a mask and possibly a hard hat, I decided to call the Health and Safety department. Someone came immediately to inspect and ordered the men (both verbally and later by letter) to either keep the doors shut or erect a plastic tunnel (I was beginning to feel like a sewer rat). To be fair to some of the builders (over the eighteen months there were many), they tried to be contained and were friendly and courteous. And of course my gripe wasn't with the majority of the workmen – after all they were just doing their jobs, and bloody hard and unpleasant ones at that. My resentment was directed at the hierarchy.

Most of my dealings were with the landlords' management representatives, a separate company who saw to the day-to-day running. I am sure that many of my complaints never reached the actual owners of the block, so levelling total responsibility for my nightmarish existence over several years at them may appear grossly unfair. However, I do believe that they are ultimately responsible for the block and therefore are morally obliged to ensure that everything is running as smoothly as possible. There were enough solicitors' letters sent to me at the landlords' behest that should have alerted them that there were serious problems. On the other hand, they could have been fully up to speed and sailing as close to the wind as was legally possible.

I'm not sure what I would have done if I hadn't had family and friends to offload on, although I could well see the day when I would be able to count my friends on one finger, I was that boring. It's very hard not to go into detail as even though the scenario is a nightmarish one, nevertheless there is a compulsion to pick over the minutiae with a fine toothcomb. It's fascinating. To me. No one else – family included. Of course they were tremendously loving and supportive but one Kanga drill is much like another and over the months and years, it has probably metamorphosed into a gnat. Mind you, gnats can be annoying.

My girls were not really aware of how low, and close to losing it completely I was, as I didn't want to burden them any more than I already was with my hysterical accounts of each new outrage. I was frequently in tears, which upset them greatly, so I kept the full extent of my feelings from them. They had their own problems to deal with and I had my duty as their mother to be supportive to them when they needed me. Children are funny though. They rarely turn to their nearest and dearest in times of crisis, preferring to discuss intimate details of their marital problems with a distant cousin of the postman, or maybe a gay friend. I am the same.

My mother was always the last to know – partly because my problems gave her sleepless nights and occasional uncontrollable nervous facial tics. She used to say to me, "I can't bear even your little finger to be hurt." She had been amazingly calm and practical when I broke up with Dan – I don't think I could have coped if she'd been upset too. She *was* upset, of course, but not so that I felt guilty about her as well. Indeed, she was very down to earth about the whole thing, "Oh, he'll be back. He loves you. He tells me all the time. You'll see, he'll be back."

I didn't bother to say that *I* left Dan. I liked the matter of fact attitude, the 'geeing me up' tone. I even began to believe he would come back after his much needed break.

Rebecca had announced her engagement to a city chap called Warner. She'd met him in her brother-in-law Gerry's wine bar where she worked in the evenings. Her sister, Susie, who didn't need to work as Gerry had several bars and restaurants, would sit on the other side of the bar in her Gucci outfit whilst Rebecca would be in the loo, cleaning up the city boys' vomit. There was a lot of it too, the result of drinking too many slammers in the lunch hour. The ambulance had to be called on more than one occasion apparently, so it was a lively sort of place.

Like Susie and Laura, Rebecca had trained to be a dancer. Whilst her sisters concentrated solely on classical ballet, Rebecca wanted to study drama as well, so she was accepted at a prestigious Stage School. She loved every moment of her time there. Such was her keenness that she would be up and ready to go every morning long before the alarm went. She did well in her exams, particularly political studies, but her Grade A results didn't sway her from wishing to pursue a career in ballet and drama. And she did indeed get film and television work. However, her finest hour was appearing on stage at the London Coliseum with Rudolph Nureyev. But, sadly, like all dancers and actresses who haven't become a household name, she had to supplement her income with menial work – as indeed Laura was doing in Los Angeles – and you can't get more menial than scraping the vomit of the rich off lavatory walls. To be fair, Susie hated seeing her sister doing this stomach churning work, but Rebecca insisted that she didn't mind – and anyway it was all good experience for an actress. She was never able to use the 'good experience' in a future horror movie however, as Warner came into the bar and decided to take her away from it all.

Warner was twenty-six and lived in Kent, near Tunbridge Wells, as did so many of the other traders who worked in the City. He was one of the so-called whizz kids (riding high at twenty-four but burnt out at thirty-four) so I wasn't too keen. I would never have let Rebecca know my feelings in a million years though, as I loved my baby with a passion.

The wedding took place just a few weeks after Dan and I had parted, so I was in a fragile state, but determined not to let it show. The ceremony was held in a pretty church in a Kent village, followed by a reception in a fairytale castle close by. Rebecca looked breathtakingly beautiful and very happy, so any reservations that I'd had went on hold. I took Kieran along (that being the first time we'd seen each other in years) as Rebecca had always been fond of him. A number of people mistook him for Dan (there was a strong resemblance) but he took it all in his stride. When asked what he'd been up to, he replied, "Touring. And we're about to make a new album." He got so carried away with his new persona that he asked Rebecca at the reception if he could play the piano after the toasts.

Rebecca and Warner moved into a nineteenth century picture-book cottage and Rebecca settled into her new life readily, all thoughts of playing Ophelia out of the window. She was the perfect wife – indeed, she would be known to press a suit at 5 a.m. if it was so required of her. Occasionally, as can happen, Warner would forget to leave her any money for shopping, so she would have to eke out whatever leftovers there were, frequently going without herself so that he could have something after a hard day's shouting.

I visited once a week, so I was aware of what was going on but I couldn't say anything because she was in total denial about the situation, fiercely loyal and didn't want me to know (even though she knew deep down that I did). She had been married for a couple of years and Warner was staying out later and later. The days that I went seemed to coincide with Warner forgetting to leave shopping money, so I made sure that I took over our 'lunch' (bread, coffee, washing up liquid, toilet rolls, leg of pork) and I always left enough for bus fares otherwise she had to walk miles down a lonely road. I would pretend that it was for flowers as we silently looked at her well stocked gardens, "A few more daffodils in that corner, maybe."

Inevitably the marriage broke down and Rebecca met her 'angel' Sean, who not only rescued her from her miserable existence (and it was far more miserable than I had suspected), but also gave her back her self-esteem.

# CHAPTER NINE

I was asked to interview Jools Holland. I've known him since his days presenting the *Tube* (still one of the most innovative rock programmes ever to hit the small screen, in my opinion). When I first met Jools he had just bought a barber's shop – one of the old saloon types with cut-throat razors and hot towels. Jools was thinking of introducing a few medical supplies also as, back in the twenties, barbers were often trained to deal with minor injuries.

"I might get a bucket of leeches, they're good for mending nasty cuts – those razors can be pretty lethal. Short back and sides, whiskers off and a couple of leeches on your chin – all for a fiver. Can't be bad!"

Some years ago Jools moved to Blackheath where, for fun, he designed a studio with a railway station exterior. Everybody thought the station was real (some people even queued outside the 'pretend' ticket office muttering things like 'British Rail, it gets worse every day. Wonder what the excuse is this time – feathers blocking lines? Train derailed by pigeon droppings?') Jools clearly had yet another talent then, but it would be some years later before it became generally known.

I had seen magazine features and a television programme on Jools' latest foray into the world of design and architecture and was deeply impressed with the classically inspired building that was taking shape in the station's sidings. Palladian grandeur that would house Studio 2, equipped with the latest state of the art recording technology. Nothing at all like the shed in Bradford's station sidings.

I was curious to see it. Who wouldn't be, and I wasn't disappointed as it was indeed a work of art. Albeit on a smaller scale, the Parthenon appeared to be rising from the Blackheath ashes. This was going to be something splendid with many innovative features, as Jools doesn't just copy an idea. As songwriter Ray Davies is inspired by great works of art, Jools is inspired by great architecture. Not that he doesn't appreciate art, as his station studio could be mistaken for an art gallery, with the walls covered in pictures – and I'm not talking the 'Day Trip to Bognor for 5/-' variety.

Jools is best known for his long running and immensely successful TV series *Later With Jools Holland* but he goes on the road regularly with his Rhythm and Blues Band.

"One of the things I like very much is going out on tour and having a frenzy and taking this army of musicians there, and then once I get weary of that I spend the rest of my time in television studios – with lots of musicians there. I enjoy travelling around but I think at the root, what I've been looking for all the time, is a song or a piece of music that will get me excited. It's a bit like a drug addict but my drug is the music. So I'll travel anywhere in the world and stay up all hours just to find that moment of truth in a piece of music. And then once you find it, what a thrill and you want to do it again and again."

"So when do you find time to work on 'The Parthenon'?"

"I do it in my sleep, that's why it's turned out a bit like a Palladian villa; it *was* supposed to be a left luggage office."

When the Talk programme finally met its demise I was very upset as I was beginning to feel slightly human again in that I was fully occupied and therefore not able to wallow in self-indulgent pity all the time. I hadn't minded that the money, as usual, was barely enough to cover the cost of my expenses as I was enjoying feeling creative again (and my editing *was* very 'creative'). I was drinking too much as well so that only served to plunge me back into the abyss. I could only afford the sort of wine that you think twice about even cooking with, thus my hangovers were so bad that if I could have crawled out of bed I would have taken myself off to the

Middlesex Hospital's A&E department. As it was I had to lie there with not only drilling *in* my head, but also drilling above my head.

I had almost finished my course with Linda but she felt that I should continue to see someone as I wasn't ready to go it alone. I really didn't want to, as we both knew that so much at the root of my 'depression' was beyond my control. She conceded that I was fully cognizant of all the facts and didn't therefore need help in finding out why I was unhappy, but possibly I needed help in learning how to cope with things. I knew what it would take to improve the quality of my life. Nothing would make me 'get over' Dan completely, so that *was* just one of those things I would have to learn to live with, but everything else was solvable and therefore a new 'attitude' wasn't the answer. I did agree to go and see the next counsellor as I thought it wouldn't do any harm to have two counsellors testify to my state of mind if I had to go to court.

I went to Bob's only a couple of times as he began to get *too* up close and personal for my liking. I didn't want to hear things like, "Are you worried that men won't find you as attractive now you're getting older?"

I hadn't, before I went to him. So in fact, seeing him has now given me more things to worry about.

I rang Kieran to reassure myself that time was still on my side and he came round that evening bearing unusual gifts – a bundle of wage packets, a half drunk bottle of wine and a thong. He said that the wage packets were to put jewellery in for customers at Portobello Road; the wine was for us both so he'd had his share already and the thong he'd bought from Tesco. I said he'd picked up the girl it had come off from Tesco, more like. We watched a film about killer bees, which even Kieran found absorbing as normally his concentration goes after the first twenty minutes, which means we never see the ending of anything. He did ask if we could skip the credits though, as he didn't want to have to sit through all the names of the bees.

Dominic also rang me that evening, so it looked like I needn't worry about Bob's myopia. I was worried, however, that my *stock* was looking increasingly less attractive with age, as the best things had long gone. I had to somehow keep it topped up.

I spent a lot of time traipsing around charity shops in the hope that I might pick up the odd bargain for my stand in the Portobello Road. I couldn't give it up, even though some weeks the profit was as little as ten pounds after expenses, as I needed the cash flow that it generated. I felt so guilty about making money from these worthy causes, however, that I always took piles of my non-vintage things in to compensate, as they would generate the same amount of money. I also found another way of salving my conscience, which was to offer my services to a branch of Help The Aged and value things for them – of course I never bought from there as that wouldn't have been ethical (there were some great things that I would have loved to have though, but at least I made certain that no one else would get them for nothing either). Naturally the takings went through the roof, as the good people who worked there didn't have a clue whether something was Chippendale or chipboard. The dealers were apparently very disgruntled at the price rises.

Dan once took dozens of his seventies stage clothes into an Oxfam shop but they were rejected on the grounds that 'no one wanted that sort of stuff any more.' I tried to explain that the sweat marks alone were collectors' items, but to no avail.

I once bought a pair of Margaret Thatcher's beige court shoes in a charity shop (her secretary took them in, apparently), and I was amused to note that the left foot had a definite swing to the right. I've still got them somewhere.

I always worry about the charity shops that never seem to have anything on their shelves other than wooden gazelles and useless bric-a-brac. And it's always a mystery – why piles of saucers? I can only hope that anything of value is sent to auction and doesn't end up in some phoney aid worker's back pocket. That still doesn't answer the saucer question though.

Although I missed being able to buy in decent antiques shops and markets, I have never been one to buy at auction. Most dealers I know go to at least one a week and for some, auctions are their only source of getting stock. Salerooms – particularly the grander ones like Sotheby's and Christie's – can be rather daunting, especially to new buyers. A good introduction to the world of nodding and scratching (although I've never seen anyone get lumbered with an item they didn't want through hay fever) is to pay a few visits to a local auction where things are more casual and relaxed. Possibly not quite as relaxed as the one a friend of mine once went to in Kent. It appeared that the auctioneer was an unwitting comedy act (appreciated only by my friend; the locals took it all in their stride). The bidding started and the ambient noise grew louder rather than subsiding. After ten minutes of trying to make himself heard over the screams of a baby, the auctioneer suggested that a nappy change might do the trick. While the mother took his advice, he made himself a cup of tea from a kettle at his side. Then a woman bidding for a set of dining chairs hesitated at £120.

"Are they worth it?" she asked him.

He replied, "Most definitely, but do go and ask your husband (who was waiting outside) whether you *should* go any higher. We'll wait for you."

I can't see that happening in Bond Street, somehow.

Bidding can be a tedious affair. Waiting around until the particular lot you've earmarked comes up should be informative, but why a *Tiepolo* failed to find a buyer and yet a photograph of Virginia Woolf's mother sold for £14,300 is irrelevant and only mildly interesting when you have a goal in mind. Will there be lots of competition? Will you be the successful bidder? Will you get carried away and pay far more than you meant to? When is your lot (checking the catalogue for the hundredth time) coming up? Some customers leave bids with the auctioneer if they cannot make the sale, but then of course there is no chance to change your mind at the eleventh hour. People who do get carried away easily should perhaps choose this method. After all, it's one thing to pick up a piano at fifty quid for your seven-year old to practise on, but at five hundred it's a drag when he switches to the mouth organ.

At the other end of the spectrum are the ubiquitous car boot sales. I have mixed feelings about these compelling events in that whilst there are definitely bargains to be had, I simply cannot cope with the bun fight as the stallholders are unloading. There are always several dealers at these stalls and some of them are very aggressive, so I would rather not take part in this undignified scramble. This of course means that real bargains are snapped up first thing, but so what? There are dozens of other wonderful bargains to be had, albeit a set of pans for a fiver or bathroom scales for fifty pence.

The weeks dragged drearily by. I was barely ticking over financially and since the Talk radio slot had gone, I was feeling unmotivated. I made a few half-hearted attempts at securing more work, but the truth was that I just wasn't feeling creative, so rather than submit inferior stuff, I concentrated on buying. I covered many miles – most of them on foot – but at least I reckoned it was keeping me fit so I didn't mind. But it was deadly dull. I would arrive home after these hikes literally worn out so after something to eat and a vat of wine, I would slump in front of the television most evenings. Frighteningly, I got to know the names of the characters in *Eastenders* and *Coronation Street* and would even ring my mother up for a blow-by-blow update should I ever miss one of the episodes. Sad.

Dan's solicitor was still sending silly letters about things of which I had no knowledge so Dominic was well and truly earning his legal aid fees. We had become quite close by now even though it was perhaps unethical to have got so involved. We hadn't repeated the condoms experiment again as I had lost my libido along with my creative aspirations. At least he didn't mind too much and he admitted that he often lost his. Did it coincide with losing his power of speech, I wondered? He thought it did. I can only hope that he has the biggest hard-on the day we do finally get to go to court.

I had to force myself to go to dinner parties and the odd event – although the invitations were rare these days as a soon-to-be (hopefully) divorcee, maybe lining up a new relationship (possibly with the hostess's husband) is not at the top of a party list. My truest and dearest friends didn't think like that as they are and have been, along with my family, my life-support. Particularly after my second bottle of wine. There have also been very kind people who would be mortified to think that I wasn't including them in my roll of honour, as they have listened patiently to my floods stories and held my hand when life without Dan seemed too much to contemplate. But that was part of the problem, I suppose. They were almost too nice. Real friends hold up a mirror; gently help you to confront your own flaws without condemning you. Marilyn (what would I do without you, eh?) has said on more than one occasion, "The trouble is Lily, you're far too sensitive."

"No I'm not!" I snap back. She's right of course. But then she is, too. Maybe it takes one to know one. She has also said that I'm very judgemental. I am. I put it down to my northern roots. Lily Blunt. I must try to be more Regents Park – and there are plenty of roots to choose from there.

My ex-husband and his wife organised regular 'net-working' parties and I did go to one or two of those. The idea was to mix people in show business with business investors as there were plenty of musicians or actors with good ideas who needed backing, just as there were star-struck entrepreneurs with money to burn. Many successful collaborations came about as a result of these glamorous champagne fuelled get-togethers. It was always very amusing to see people's reactions when I told them that Patrick was my ex-husband, particularly as I was made a fuss of by both Patrick and Carmen.

I took Kieran to one event which was held in a marquee in the garden of an ambassador friend of theirs. It was late autumn so the marquee had central heating as it was a bitterly cold evening. Kieran decided to have a look around the unlit grounds ('just black bushes everywhere'), so he didn't see the swimming pool. He came back dripping from head to toe. Sadly, I wasn't amused or concerned as I'd been pissed off with him from the moment he'd arrived to pick me up. He was over an hour late ('I had a wall to build'), he was covered in brick dust and had oil all over his hands ('the car broke down'). I wasn't surprised when I saw the heap he'd selected to go to a rather swish 'do' in. I'm not a snob but I do think, when he had eight other cars to choose from, he could at least have picked one with windows. We broke down two more times. Worst of all though, when I commented on the fact that he hadn't even bothered to shave (as if that would have saved the day), from his pocket he pulled out a Bic disposable razor and began to scrape off his two-day growth. At the entrance to the marquee. So you see Kieran, shivering over a tiny oil heater was too little, too late.

We didn't see each other for quite a while after that (Kieran was just as pissed off at my 'over-reaction') but I could have done with his services a few days later when my hot water suddenly became a thin trickle. The pressure on the cold was also reduced but nowhere near as drastic. I really didn't want to have to call in the landlords' plumber, but as I couldn't afford an independent one I had no alternative. Fortunately, one of the men I'd known for years came and he fiddled about with various pipes under the sink before telling me in a low voice (in case I was bugged, I presume) that because my system was connected to the one in the new flat/office next door, my pressure had dropped as a result.

I presumed he meant that this outcome would have been predicted. So I rang the powers that be and they agreed to send an inspector round. I was told that the pressure reduction had nothing to do with the new flat and that it was simply a case of the pipes having corroded over the years and, as my flat was at the bottom of the building, 'all the muck and crap' had built up. The only solution was to have a whole new system.

Hang on. A whole new system? Pipes throughout my flat

would have to be ripped out and after that upheaval, new ones would be installed? How many men and months would that take if a simple leak in a bath took four men and eight days? I would probably have to move out. With my furniture. Red alert. I called the water board.

A representative came out immediately. He examined everything thoroughly, including the pipes course through the corridor and out into the back yard where they joined a maze of tubes and ducting. His assessment was that the problem did arise more than likely from the new system installed next door. To be certain, he would of course have to take a look. However, the work had gone on hold, so the doors to the flat/office were locked. No one was available to discuss the matter so I reluctantly had to let the technician go, but he promised to return if I could make arrangements to get in the place.

I received a letter from the management stating that the new flat/office was on a separate water supply from mine – as indeed was the rest of the building –and therefore the fault would appear to be in my flat. Would I confirm that I would be happy for the contractor to gain access to my apartment to undertake the necessary works.

I couldn't risk it. So for the last two years I've had virtually no hot water. The silly thing is that because it takes forty minutes to fill the kitchen sink, I have had several floods. Obviously I can't stand over the sink for that length of time, so I do something else and if I'm in another room, I forget about it. There are times when I can't stand it, but then I think of the alternative.

# CHAPTER TEN

My mother had been suffering with a painful hip for almost a year and finally she was going into hospital for a replacement. Although she was a National Health patient, her doctor had managed to get her a place in a small private hospital.

She was thrilled to find that she had a spacious room, with views across the Airedale Valley, all to herself. I stayed at her flat a few miles away, so visiting was easy. Well, not that easy in fact. I couldn't walk there as seven miles up and down big hills (and there are lots of them) turns into about twenty. And I couldn't get a taxi – not so much because I couldn't afford it (I couldn't), but the local fleet of two had to be booked days in advance to be certain of securing one. To call one from Bradford city centre would mean it would have clocked up my entire bus fare budget just getting to me, let alone going on to the hospital. The bus stop was near the flat, so the first leg of the journey was quick. The next part could be. However, the timetable was a work of fiction, so 'on the hour' sometimes meant forty-five past the hour. This invariably meant I missed the next bus, which could mean another long wait (I'll never grumble about the capital's bus services again). Despite all this, the views were magnificent, the air clean and at least the sheep didn't 'jump the queue' as is the natural law in London.

After all these years, I cannot get used to that. It's a hangable offence in the north. If a ninety year old with heavy bags and calipers is behind a big strapping lad, she/he will wait patiently in line rather than trying to pull rank and 'push in'. The big strapping lad will more than likely let her/him go first as, on the whole, they do have manners. I'm not of course talking school kids en masse here, as they are utterly oblivious to anything but who can say FUCK the loudest, as most of them appear to be deaf. Asking your best friend/worst enemy who is sitting next to you 'What are you fucking doing this evening?' is not a shouting issue (*unless* your ears don't work).

My mother's operation was fine and the next day she was sitting up in bed, her hair done, her lipstick on and wearing a pale blue jacket trimmed with angora – the sort that undulates with the slightest movement. She looked positively radiant.

"I feel great. Mr. Pearson (surgeon) was marvellous, I didn't feel a thing."

"That's good, he'd have lost his job if you had."

She laughed, replying, "You know what I mean."

I didn't actually. Did she really think she ought to feel a dull sawing?

"It's just like an hotel," she continued enthusiastically. "The food's fantastic. Last night I had a huge piece of beef – and it was so tender – carrots, peas, fried onions, mashed potatoes, and they're so generous with the butter. After, there was apple pie and thick cream. Wonderful."

If she had been a private patient, I might have cynically suggested that stuffing patients full of all that artery clogging food would ensure a return visit. (I'll lay ten to one the heart bypass ward was full). Then again, the menu was typical northern fare.

I met one of her doctors the next day, a temporary locum called Keith. We got chatting and I learned that he lived in Bradford but his home was in a small village in Sussex. He'd been at university in Bradford and decided he liked the place, and more or less stayed on. He was currently working in geriatrics but his ambition was to be a psychiatrist.

"Nice knowing you," I said, backing out of the room quickly.

My mother was mystified at my abrupt departure when I spoke to her on the 'phone later that evening.

"Why on earth did you go like that? Keith was sorry you left. I could tell. You never know, he might be nice to go out with."

"Mother, he's going to be a psychiatrist, we don't like them. They take their trousers off in public – remember? Guy?"

"Guy was lovely," she replied disgustedly.

Some people do have short memories.

"And what are you talking about? He was decent – he was in your bed covered up, his clothes were on the chair. Keith is charming."

"But he's probably married."

"He's not. I asked him."

I groaned. "I'll bet you've told him everything about me."

"I have," was the triumphant reply.

"You needn't think I'm going to pick you up after that, you can hop home."

We then had a row because she thought my attitude was ridiculous as a doctor would be interested in 'what you've been through'. I explained that some psychiatrists weren't even interested in what their own patients had been through, let alone the daughter of someone who'd had their hip replaced.

I had to pick her up of course. Keith was sitting with her when I arrived. She gave me a knowing look and went into the bathroom to 'pack a few things'.

"Don't forget those lovely fluffy towels!" I shouted. Keith laughed and jokily handed me the bedside lamp.

"At these prices she needs a few perks." He continued, "Your mother is very nice and she is so proud of you, you know."

Didn't I know it. I couldn't count the number of times she had gone to the local paper about me.

I thought it was incredible how my mother could dictate what went in to the particular feature, almost word for word. Here's a typical example:

'Lily, the daughter of Mrs. Dorothy Francis of Shipley, first became hooked on a career in the entertainment world when she was a teenager and a member of the Students Jazz

Club. She had her first taste of show business when she became Rag Queen. Her mother, a former court usher said, "She is a really hard worker and has done very well." '

The court usher, rag queen stuff, was prerequisite padding. My mother had got it into her head that being a parochial rag queen for a day was the pinnacle of my career. It was certainly the 'achievement' she was most proud of. I'll bet even if Madonna had recorded one of my songs, the newspaper would feel obliged to write, "Former Bradford Rag Queen, Lily Francis, daughter of former court usher, Dorothy Francis..."

Keith asked when I was going back to London. I said I'd stay just another week or so as my mother was already amazingly mobile. He then asked if we could meet for a drink before I left. He was very attractive – and older than most of the others – so I agreed. We met a couple of nights later. He picked me up from my mother's as he wanted to see how she was getting on. Naturally she was seated so, rather endearingly, he crouched down beside her.

"He's lovely," my mother mouthed behind his back as we left.

We went to the White house Restaurant on Baildon Moors. The best restaurant in Yorkshire, in my opinion. The food is fantastic and the views (from every window) were stunning.

The White House wasn't always such an epicurean delight though. I remember when it was a humble tea shop (good cakes, mind). I took my children there when they were still quite young – not yet teenagers. I said I thought it would be a good idea to walk to it from a point visible from the restaurant, as it didn't seem that far. However, I hadn't reckoned with the dips (*not* visible from the dining area), which were filled with ditches and small woods. Susie twisted her ankle but it was too far to go back so we had no alternative but to press on. Up, rather, as the final leg was up a steep bank. The journey took over two hours when it had looked like no more than a fifteen minute gambol.

We were grateful for the tea and custard slices, but our pleasure was spoilt by two insufferable louts at the next table who behaved a bit like those 'deaf' schoolchildren I've already mentioned. Why weren't they in a greasy spoon instead of this genteel establishment? It certainly seemed odd that they would want to risk their mates seeing them.

The old dears who ran the tearoom obviously didn't dare ask them to leave, but they made certain that they got the thinnest slices of cake in the hope that they would gobble them up quickly and go. My girls were almost in tears when they saw the tiny pieces, "We know they're horrible boys, Mummy, but look at the mean little slices they've been given."

Anyway, they didn't wolf them down and continued to annoy everyone. Now even though we had tramped across fields, crossed becks and fought our way through malevolent gorse bushes, we still managed to look like a charming, well-mannered family. So everyone was completely taken by surprise when, in my best BBC accent, I loudly said, "I wish they'd shut the fuck up." There was a nervous giggle from the boys behind but it did the trick and for the rest of the tea break they did indeed shut the fuck up.

I was feeling very apprehensive – remember I'm not used to this dating lark (I don't count Dominic and Kieran, as they're more chums than lovers), so I ordered a simple prawn with rice dish as I didn't want to be chewing great wodges of food whilst we were talking. I felt uncomfortable under Keith's thoughtful gaze - any minute he would nod knowingly and write a letter to a friend, I imagined. I knew that I was acting very unnaturally, girlie and coy, twiddling my hair and things. I was also drinking too much, very dangerous in stilettos – the quaint stone steps had been difficult enough to negotiate sober. It's weak and pathetic to turn to drink but it does make the drilling pleasanter, Eastenders more Chekhov and a prospective lover not such a big deal. I didn't want to lose this one though, so I ordered strong black coffee instead of the proffered wine.

"Go on, have another glass," coaxed Keith seductively.

"Better not. One barrel a night's my limit." Men. They just don't help, do they?

As we just happened to be passing his door (quelle surprise), on the way back to my mother's, he wondered if I'd like a nightcap. I knew I shouldn't but I really did like him and the tenuous link with my mother made it feel safe somehow.

Three sips later and we were discussing my favourite subject – condoms. One minute he was telling me about the new wing of St. Luke's Hospital, the next he was undoing his zip. Help. Where had I gone wrong? Very matter of factly, he said he didn't use condoms but there was no need to worry, he knew what he was doing. I presumed he meant 'Trust me, I'm a doctor'.

I was so amazed at this arrogant and ignorant assumption that my jaw dropped. Mistaking this for lust and before you could say 'pork sword', he had whipped out a defiantly bendy penis and was advancing towards my open mouth with it. Pushing him away, I said, "You don't do condoms because you're a doctor? Well I don't do oral sex because I'm a vegetarian."

My mother could never understand why I didn't want to discuss my night out with him. Or why I didn't want to see him again. I went home a couple of days later because my mother was able to walk with just a walking stick. We had even tackled one of the steepest hills in Bradford leading up to the moors. My mother was putting on her heeled shoes, which really worried me as the operation had obviously turned her brain.

"You can't wear high heeled court shoes to climb hills and cross bumpy moors."

"I'm not wearing *flat* shoes," she said in a disparaging voice. "You never know who I might meet. One of my policeman friends."

"Is that where burglars go then? Baildon Moors, the seedy underbelly of Bradford? Ooh Mummy, I'm scared. I don't want to go now."

Normally my mother would have laughed at the thought of the flying squad and Ken, her dog-handler friend, staking out Mr. Robinson's ice cream van and a solitary sheep pen, but as she was feeling guilty about her shoes she gave me a withering look instead.

"I sometimes wonder if you're my daughter, the things you say. You don't get it from me, or your father."

And with that we set off to cross the tufty moors, me in my brogues, my mother in something far daintier.

When I returned to London I was distressed to find that the back yard had been filled with scaffolding. Part of my flat was in this area so I really did feel as though I was 'sealed in' now. I still had all the other monstrous rigging around me, so it wasn't good. One of the steel poles had gone through the lavatory window, breaking an art deco stained glass panel. I did claim for this but, as usual, it took ages to resolve. Later the process was repeated again in a bedroom. Nothing of mine was damaged but as there was a huge gaping hole, the glass had to be replaced immediately. So more men trampling their dirty boots through my immaculate flat (immaculate in the circumstances), leaving the walls stained with black fingerprints – impossible to remove completely – but not even worth complaining about, as I had learnt over time.

Many of the other statutory tenants were also experiencing problems but not to the extent that I was, as I was the only one living on such a prime site. Also, now that most of the tenants in my section of the block had left, the apartments could be subjected to makeovers without fear of complaints from anyone who mattered – and I certainly wasn't one of *them*.

As if things couldn't get worse, I discovered to my horror that I had a small bald patch on top of my head by my parting, right at the front. I knew that it was probably stress related and that my hair would grow back, but for a long time I had to camouflage it.

Dan's solicitors had written accusing us of dragging our heels regarding the divorce. We were indeed contributing to this protracted affair but only because we were trying to obtain information that wasn't forthcoming. Dominic suggested that rather than accept the other side's word as fact, we should see written proof. This can take a long time coming, naturally, but it was what didn't come that concerned us.

Eventually a date was set, as apparently legal aid would not cover the detailed and exhaustive investigation that was needed to resolve things satisfactorily, so a line had to be drawn somewhere. We had three weeks to wrap it all up.

Meanwhile, Dominic still found time to play. Literally. Fancying himself as a singer/songwriter in the Bob Dylan mould (I really did think he was too old for me sometimes), he had started carrying his guitar around with him.

"Please don't bring it to court, will you?" I begged.

"I thought Dan and I might do a duet together," he teased.

He did bring it, however, the following Saturday to Portobello. He took the antiques thing too far, though, when he turned up wearing 1930's funeral director's trousers and a First World War grandfather shirt which he wore with one sleeve rolled up and the cuff of the other dangling past his fingertips. His guitar was round his neck in a 'ready to go' position.

"You're not going to serenade my customers, are you?" I asked. Then before he could answer, I repeated, "You are NOT going to serenade my customers." I hadn't expected Dominic to turn up at Portobello, of all places. I didn't go to his office with my piano.

He replied in soothing tones, "I think a bit of background music would be fun for your customers."

"They want to buy Rolex watches, not have fun," (and the prices of my neighbour's Rolex's certainly were more conducive to having a heart attack than to breaking into a soft shoe shuffle.)

Not one to be thwarted, he said, "I'll go upstairs, then."

The café was still not a good venue as people I knew went

up there. I wasn't sure that his odd, clenched teeth style delivery would go down well with everyone.

"Don't tell anyone that you're my solicitor, or that you even know me. Please. I'll never see you again after I'm divorced if you do."

He laughed good-humouredly and strummed quietly to another neighbour who pretended not to hear him, before climbing the stairs to the café.

"And don't have a collection plate!" I shouted after him.

He stayed there for three hours. The owner obviously thought it was good for business as there was a steady stream going up to hear the 'new busker'. One of my regular customers said, "Your solicitor is really good, isn't he? He should bill himself 'The Singing Solicitor'.

"Sweetheart, they love me," he said triumphantly at the end of his marathon set. "I'm coming back next week."

"I'll have you barred."

"Disbarred," he corrected, handing me a sticky bun.

He didn't take any notice of me and continued to amuse the crowds for another couple of weeks until he lost interest.

Occasionally I went to a market in Birmingham to give my stock a change of scenery. It attracted buyers and sellers from as far afield as Glasgow and London. I usually went with my Sandown Park friend, Robert, as we shared a stand and kept one another amused on what would otherwise have been an horrendous coach trip. Don't get me wrong, the coach trip was well organised and pleasantly supervised, but the idea of a three-hour journey with a bunch of antiques dealers can be depressing, as the only topic of conversation on these outings revolves around antiques. Thankfully, many people sleep all the way there as we leave at 4.30 a.m. (although I do wish Robert wouldn't point out the ones who look like stunned cod with their mouths open), and we arrive in time to have a fortifying cup of warm water – it's coffee apparently, or so I'm told – before the doors open. The crush to get into the hall is quite frightening and if you get through with merely bruises and the odd fractured rib you've done very well.

The dilemma each time is whether to sell a bit first and then look around or whether to buy first and sell later. One tends to sell more in the initial rush, but then again if there are any bargains they most certainly will have gone if one leaves the buying until later. I had the compensation from my beautiful stained glass window, so I decided to invest it in the hope that it would generate more money. I thought it best to join in the treasure hunt straight away – particularly as my stock wasn't going to be pounced on with delight, either first thing or last thing.

I was immediately rewarded with picking up a fabulous forties shagreen – or sharkskin – handbag. "It's ten pounds, love." I was so taken aback by this as I'd expected it to be at least a hundred pounds (and *that* would have been cheap) that I didn't answer. "Oh, alright, you've twisted my arm, it can be seven." Before she'd a chance to offer it for a fiver, I quickly paid her and moved on, feeling quite guilty. On the other hand, if she was that stupid why should I worry? There's more to antiques than just making a quick profit (however small), learning the value and appreciating the quality and workmanship is definitely more rewarding.

Anyway, that was a good start but it could just as easily have gone downhill, as I do tend to buy a lot of things that I like instead of simply commercial items. I dare say the bottle of 'Holy Water' won't be to everyone's taste (Robert said later it could be to his taste with a drop of gin in it), but it's so kitsch. I thought the label said 'Holy Water – from Lourdes', but it's actually from Leeds. I can't think of anything holy from Leeds apart from my mother who goes to chapel every Sunday.

A small crowd had gathered in one corner of the hall as someone was getting a thrashing – he was probably trying to nick something and had got caught. It can be such an intimidating market as it's full of the toughest dealers. I once saw a dealer smash all his *own* stock in sheer frustration at a car that had parked in front of his stall all morning (cars are not supposed to stay in the hall beyond a reasonable unloading period), despite frequent requests for its removal over the tannoy. This was *after* he'd tried unsuccessfully to strangle the driver, incidentally.

Yet despite the battlefield ambience, I really do look forward to the event as there are some very nice dealers who go there too. I always learn something new from one or other of these interesting individuals, usually over a coffee and an excellent cream gateau in a café across the way. I learnt on this particular trip that Hitler cheated on his tax returns in 1926.

I bought a few more bits and pieces, nothing exciting but hopefully saleable and they would at least give my tired old stock a bit of a boost. The day ends as it began, only the coach is now extremely hot from several hours in the sun. After the initial excitement of showing off any bargains to each other, the same people fall asleep again and the same mouths drop open. I wonder whether to sprinkle a little Holy Water into them to revive them but decide against it as the chatter is definitely worse. As it is, one man drones on for the whole of the journey about this dealer and that dealer. I'd like to hit him on the head with the bottle of Holy Water, never mind pour it down his throat. And that's what Birmingham does for you; if you can't join 'em, beat 'em!

# CHAPTER ELEVEN

There were shards of broken glass outside of my front door this morning – fine shards easy to miss visually but lethal if trodden on in flimsy slippers (and I do frequently go out first thing in the morning to check for my post which has been going astray of late). Naturally I immediately rang the management company – *and* put it in writing – and was informed that someone would contact me about it. No one did contact me so I had to clear up the glass and other rubbish myself. I finally received a letter saying that the contractors who carried out the work resulting in this dangerous mess would be clearing it away. Three days on, after the event I wrote back, 'I am tired of being fobbed off (either that, or no one takes any notice of you), so I have had to clean the debris away myself. I was tempted to dump it on your desk but I have been advised by my solicitor to keep it as evidence.'

The noise from the back yard was so bad that it reached a new level of insanity. The metal fire escape was being pulled down as part of the refurbishment scheme and it was scheduled to last 'approximately'six weeks. Two years on, it was still in progress. During this time I would suffer severe chest problems from the choking dust that crept into my flat. (The head porter suffered with similar chest infections throughout). My doctor attributed them directly to the longstanding works and again said he would be prepared to testify in court.

One of the other aspects, whilst not serious to my physical well being, nevertheless did my head in – the constant shouting, swearing and singing of boring out of tune songs at the tops of voices. A cacophony of machinery noise and raucous human rabble smashing into my senses day in and day out, unremitting apart from a few hours on Saturday and Sunday. I rarely accepted invitations to go out on these precious, silent days. Not that I was sleeping better as I had now got into the habit of waking up at the slightest sound, thanks to years of 'ear bashing', so I'm lucky if I have more than four hours sleep a night, to this day.

It would all have been so much easier if I had a partner (indeed, it probably would not have got personal at all had I been living with someone) but I wasn't about to get involved with someone who could protect me from the landlords on the one hand but wouldn't be prepared to protect me from a sexually transmitted disease on the other. Incidentally, that unintended euphemism reminds me of the time I had two warts, one on each thumb, strangely, and my HIV doctor friend said I should have them removed. He said that he would do it and to pop into his clinic at the Hammersmith Hospital. I hadn't thought at the time that 'his clinic' was a genito-urinary one, although I should have realised that it would have been something to do with sexually transmitted diseases. The bewildered looks on the faces of the patients when I came out with both my thumbs bandaged were something I'll never forget.

Dominic had begun downsizing his company to save money. His current partner was leaving to start up on his own so Dominic would have to carry all administration costs from now on. He rented offices in a block occupied by other legal firms and had the use of various facilities including the communal receptionist. However, his secretary had to be paid for out of his own pocket. Legal secretaries don't come cheap, so Dominic decided he could manage without her. One week before my divorce was due to be heard in court. There was still so much to do. As is often the way, many things couldn't be done until the last minute, hence we (yes, I was the new unpaid secretary) worked every night, past midnight on two occasions. We didn't complete all the paperwork despite our efforts and I felt quite sick at just how unprepared we were. After all the time I'd had, not to mention three solicitors on the case.

Dominic picked me up on the morning of the hearing looking as though he'd slept in his clothes. He hadn't; he'd worked in them, all night.

"You look dreadful. And where's your tie?"

"Do I need one?" he asked in genuine surprise.

"You can't go into court in a crumpled pin striped suit, a grubby shirt and no tie, it won't look good. You should know that."

"I'll buy one."

He stopped the taxi in the Strand and nipped into a men's outfitters. He came back with two and let me choose which one the judge would like the most. Difficult choice. The one with the Cairn terriers, or the striped one? Stripes with a striped suit? He'd strobe – but still at least he could dazzle with his tie because he sure as hell wasn't going to dazzle with his filing system.

Susie and Rebecca met us at Somerset House and was I glad to see them. I hadn't had a chance to think about coming face to face with Dan after all this time – over four years – but now the moment was imminent I felt very, very nervous.

He looked older and thinner (he was probably thinking the same thing about me) and apart from his solicitor, he was on his own. I had my lovely girls in a show of strength and solidarity so I couldn't help but feel sorry for him. I still loved him and I was filled with such a deep sadness that it should have come to this.

Dan and I sat opposite each other in the courtroom, somewhat informally, around a table. Throughout the hearing, which lasted almost two hours, Dan didn't look at me once. He must have got a crick in his neck (I felt sorry for him about that too). I willed him to look at me to no avail.

The judge told us off for not presenting the papers up front and she more or less dismissed them, saying that she wasn't going to plough through them at this late hour. She accused me of getting my marriage date wrong and that I'd added a year on. That completely threw me and for a fraction of a second, I thought maybe I had. Of course I hadn't, but she had moved on by then and wasn't interested in my protestations. She appeared to hate us (the late papers thing hadn't helped, probably) and could have been mistaken for a Dan Walters fan (she was about the right age), such was her interest in everything the opposition had to say.

I was so relieved when it was all over as I really think it was one of the most horrible experiences of my life. The divorce settlement would at least ensure that no one would be after me for my money, as when it came through it would go immediately on debts.

Laura hadn't been at the court with her sisters because she was still in America looking for that elusive break. She had rented a tiny house in the Hollywood Hills with the money she earned from her two – occasionally three – jobs. During the day she worked in a designer dress shop on Melrose Avenue, frequented by A-list celebrities ('Michelle Pfeiffer is the nicest, Julia Roberts isn't') and at night as a roller skating/dancing waitress. When she got the chance she would fit in a cleaning job as well. As if all that wasn't hard enough, she had to go on foot in the early days as she couldn't afford a car. No one walks in Hollywood, as the roads are not built for pedestrians, so she got very odd looks from everyone. I think she's a star with or without Tom Cruise as her leading man.

When Laura left school at seventeen, she joined a touring Ballet Company so she managed to see something of the world before making the decision to try her luck in America. She won her green card in a lottery. Bizarre really. I think we should do things like that here. If I thought I could win, say, a driving licence (because I won't get one any other way), then I'd have a go once a week.

She had an agent who did send her to auditions and she got work from those, but not enough to sustain a Hollywood lifestyle, however frugal. So she didn't give up her day job although the night job eventually went – mainly for safety reasons as a girl walking alone at 2 a.m. is asking for trouble. She did buy herself a motorbike eventually, which for a while solved the getting from A to B problem. We were very concerned when we heard that this was her new mode of transport, as she had been more of a tutu girl than a Hell's Angel. Unsurprisingly, she did have an accident but fortunately wasn't injured. However, it shook her, so reluctantly she hung up her Byker boots and bought instead a tiny car (which by its condition didn't sound as though it was much safer than the bike).

In the two years that she was there, I never went to see her (although I did intend to) as I hate flying. I know all the arguments. I know that there are more crashes on the roads in one year in Britain than there have been in the whole of aviation history (and I'm not counting the planes that have been lost in wars). Friends have told me to just get drunk – I don't understand how a bottle of wine inside me helps to keep the plane up, something to do with dynamics, I suppose. I simply do not fancy the thought of crashing and my kidneys dangling from trees near Orly airport, or wherever.

I have of course flown, but only if absolutely forced to. Like the time Dan and I had gone to Paris on what used to be known as the 'magic bus'. Magic because it was cheap, and magic because one boarded at Victoria and apart from flexing one's sea legs crossing the channel, didn't have to move again until it landed in the centre of Paris.

Our return journey should have been just as straight forward. Due to leave at 10 p.m. we arrived at the boarding point half an hour early and took our seats, as the coach was already in. Five minutes before the departure time, some bloke came round to check tickets. When he saw ours, he ordered us off, saying that we hadn't 'checked in' so we must relinquish our seats to a couple on standby. We refused as no one had told us to do this. He said that he would call the police if we didn't. Everyone around us encouraged us to stay put and we did.

Eight gendarmes arrived ten minutes later in what was the French equivalent of a black maria. They forced everyone off the bus (guns cocked at the ready) and then surrounded

Dan and me whilst the driver ushered the rest back on. They wouldn't listen to our explanations – although I probably said rubbish like 'La plume de ma tante', as that was all I could think of in my limited schoolgirl French. I did call them 'cochons' though, under my breath. The coach pulled away and the gendarmes climbed back into their wagon and we were just left there to fend for ourselves. The bloke who had got us into this mess came over and offered to run us to the airport after he'd locked up. He spoke good English so I was able to fully vent my wrath. I told him that I didn't fly and that we couldn't wait for the next coach (he had told us before offering a lift that the next one wasn't scheduled until 9 a.m. the next morning) as Dan had a television show to do back in London. That was true. He had. Dan said that he would miss the show but I couldn't let him do that as I knew that he hated letting anyone down, particularly the rest of the band.

Andre was very chatty on the way and asked Dan what he did. When he learned who he was he almost crashed the car. "But I've seen you in Paris, it was a fantastique show. I cannot believe you are Dan Walters, in my car. You must come and stay with me the next time you come to Paris."

I couldn't believe how we'd gone from public enemy number one to best buddies in less than an hour. Dan gave him his autograph and actually thanked him for the lift. Thanked the man who was more than likely sending us to our doom.

We had a long wait at the airport. We were the only people in the lounge. I tried to sleep but Dan, who was pacing about, kept tugging at my skirt as it was riding up. There was no one to see, as I said, but it really worried him. Three hours later we finally boarded a plane to London. It was from the Arab Emirates, El Al or something. The female staff were covered from head to toe in ubiquitous black with just their beautiful expressive eyes showing. This was at the time when there had been a number of hijackings, so I was convinced that once up in the air, the robes would be thrown off to reveal a bunch of armed fanatics who would take us hostage. I wondered how much Dan Walters was worth in the eighties. It didn't bode well. Surprisingly, nothing like this happened, the staff were dignified and charming and we got home safely. But I'll never fly again.

The only other disruption on a magic bus was once when I had been to Paris with a friend – pre-Dan – and the police took off the two blokes sitting next to us at Dover. They never came back and we later learnt that live ammunition had been found in their shoes. They were apparently running away from the Foreign Legion. And I always thought one ran away *to* it!

My mother wasn't like me. She loved flying (she went up in a helicopter on her seventieth birthday) and had gone to see Laura shortly after she threw away her walking stick and funny loo seat that people who have had hip replacements are issued with. She had been to America once before, a weekend on her own in New York. This was just before her seventieth birthday as she wanted to spend that with us, but this was our present to her as it had long been her ambition to visit. We're never very surprised at the things my mother does as she has a zest for life matched only by her energy and enthusiasm. However, even we couldn't believe that she'd gone wandering around the Bronx one evening. It wasn't that she hadn't been warned to stay away from certain places. She said it was a glorious evening and everyone was so friendly sitting out on doorsteps, waving to her and shouting greetings like, 'Yoh'. She said that she came across a big group of youths but rather than feeling afraid, she went up to a couple and asked them if they could tell her where Peter Stringfellow's club was. Needless to say, these young Bronx break dancing cool dudes couldn't, but I wouldn't be surprised if there isn't perhaps a rap song along the lines of 'crazy (grand) motherfucker looking for a good time, Yoh is alright, come back any night, in your high heeled sneakers and big hat'.

Peter wasn't at his club as he was back in England. "But at least I can say I've been."

Los Angeles was a dream come true. My mother had the time of her life. Laura's letter summarises it perfectly.

"Dear Mummy,

Now that Nana has gone back to sunny Bradford, I can tell you a little of the fun we had.

On the drive from LA airport we had to go through the unsavoury area of South Central. She thought it very smart. I said that it was really dangerous. She said, 'It doesn't bother me, all the creeps and thugs I've had to deal with.'

She liked the flat, especially the pool, which reminded me of how brilliant it is even though most people have them. I told you on the phone that I've got three jobs at the moment – in this city if you don't work, there's no dole, you live under a bridge. I do realise that I'm only days away from international stardom, but until then……….. So, on Nana's first morning I offered her the choice of watching 'Cop TV' (always a good option with Nana), or coming with me to my cleaning job at an apartment on the Disney lot. She came with me. As I arrived with my mops and buckets it did strike me that some people might think it odd to take their grandmother with them on their cleaning job. I sat Nana down and started but found it difficult with the constant barrage of 'you've missed a bit' or 'you're not doing it like that, surely?' In the end we did it together, so she spent her first day in Hollywood cleaning.

As I've lived here for a while now, I know all the interesting, free, real Hollywood things to do. So I took her on the graveyard tour. The graveyards in America are fascinating; often beautiful, quiet places. And of course, most of the stars of yesteryear are there. I took a photo of her sitting on Tyrone Power's grave, as he was her pin-up. Then we went to see Jayne Mansfield, Valentino and Peter Finch ('I was never a fan but take a photo anyway'). Then we went to Forest Lawns (these are all over California). There are no graves as such, just plaques in the ground and miles of sweeping hills and statues. Michelangelo's David – a copy – is there, and there is the biggest painting in the world in a mausoleum, specially built for it. It seats one thousand people and we were the only ones there. And it's free.

We sat through the 'show' three times. Sections of the painting are revealed bit by bit. Actors' voices narrate what is on the canvas with Charlton Heston as God (wasn't he Moses?) Then the whole painting is revealed to angel voices in 'soundarama'. Fantastic. This is more Hollywood than anything else and we were on our own. Nana loved it. On the way out we passed a glass case with a crown of thorns, a little sign said 'Just like The One'.

Then it was on to Venice Beach. It's like Portobello every day, friendly people, freaky people, very bustling. Nana got chatting to some policemen of course, she said to them, 'You know Peter Sutcliffe – Ripper? Well, I had him in twice.' They were so nice, had no idea what she meant but agreed to pose for photos on their motorbikes with her perched in between, (which I enclose).

We drove down the Pacific Coast Highway to the John Paul Getty Museum in Malibu. It's on top of a cliff and built in the style of a Roman Villa. We met my ex-boyfriend Steve (who you will remember, comes from Barnsley) there and Nana was in her element with him. They talked about the areas and people they both knew. He was lovely with her ('You're too glamorous to be Laura's grandmother' to which she replied 'I know dear, and I don't dye my hair, I just put a rinse on it').

When we got back to Hollywood Steve took her for a ride on his motorbike and then we went for dinner to the 'Ol Spaghetti House', which is inside a mock brain. Of course we did a lot of the real touristy stuff, tour of the star homes, Universal Studios (where she went twenty feet up in the air on ET's bicycle) but it was the off the beaten track stuff that she really liked. LA can be daunting, dangerous and fast but Nana fitted right in. We had a lovely time. I'll phone at the weekend.

Love Laura x x x x"

# CHAPTER TWELVE

It had been unsettling seeing Dan, having to face the reality of my situation. I had to try and get some sort of sense to my life as I was spending my days battling with noise, dirt, officious bureaucracy, lack of money, ill-health and a general darkness of the soul which, if I didn't get a grip, would spiral out of control. I could see how hard it was for people for whom there was no light at the end of the tunnel. At least I could write, if I could only apply myself, and I had my family and friends. I wasn't sure I would have a home for much longer though, as I was constantly aware that I was fighting a professional body who could afford the best advice, who had the power and skill to intimidate a woman on her own. When your home is threatened, it's very, very unnerving. However, I am not a quitter, and I was brought up to abhor injustice, so I will just keep on battling. I did think it was about time I sought professional advice though – and I'm not talking Dominic. As willing as he was – and he would have done it for nothing if I couldn't get legal aid – I thought that a non-singing, hard-nosed lawyer was what I needed now.

I went first of all to see the Citizens' Advice solicitor as he can recommend a legal aid solicitor best suited to your needs. He said that it certainly sounded as though I was being harassed and gave me a couple of names to contact.

The first chap I went to see seemed to be run off his feet with asylum seekers. It didn't feel right. I waited though, as I had to give him a chance. He started to fire questions the minute I walked through his office door, not even looking at me as he scribbled notes. He said he couldn't do anything until legal aid came through but a 'green form' would take care of preliminaries. I filled this in and then told him about the suspected harassment. He laughed derisively, although he did say that they probably were harassing me, but as for the 'woman on her own' bit, that was rubbish. Rubbish because I didn't seem like someone easily intimidated. How dare he! He obviously had problems – he certainly had small feet (and you know what they say about men with small feet).

The other solicitor inspired more confidence. He agreed that it all sounded very suspicious and there was no question in his mind about it being harassment. However, proving it wasn't that easy. First though I had to apply for legal aid – he thought there would be no trouble with getting it –and we would take it from there. Meanwhile he asked me to write a list and resumé of everything that had happened. I had kept some notes but not a comprehensive diary, so it wasn't going to be easy. I didn't want to leave anything out even though just the main events were enough to make a strong case in my favour.

Again, I had to fill in a green form (which apparently entitled me to about two hours of free time with a solicitor before, and if, legal aid was granted) but at least I felt that I was finally beginning to get somewhere.

The day after the meeting I rang with most of the answers to the numerous queries and to thank him for his help so far. A few days later I had cause to ring again as there were new developments, which once again were threatening my well-being.

There had been a flood in the corridor outside of my front door whilst I was away from my flat, so I had to negotiate strategically placed buckets rapidly filling with water and at the same time, tread gingerly on the slippery, filthy linoleum (the carpet, ruined in the initial work programme some months previously, had never been replaced). Two days later the ceiling came down and all the heavy-duty pipes and wires were exposed along twenty-four feet of corridor, up to my door. Most of the lights were out so I nearly didn't see the cable that hung noose-like, low enough to loop around my head. I shudder to think what would have happened if I'd slipped on the treacherous floor.

Imagine my amazement when, after relaying this to the solicitor, he said, "Why are you ringing me again? Your time is up (the two hours 'free time'). Please don't ring me any more unless it's urgent."

The head porter had a similar reaction from one of the management team when he was nearly hit on the head by a metal pole falling from the scaffolding at the top of the building, as he was advised to 'take a photo the next time'.

I wrote a Dear John letter immediately – although I was worried that he would send me a hefty bill just for reading it – and I called the legal aid office to ask if my application could go on hold.

I was plunged into gloom thinking of how hit and miss it was, finding a good and empathetic solicitor. It wasn't that legal aid funded solicitors were necessarily a wash out. Indeed many of them are genuinely altruistic as they have to wait a long time to recoup their fees, but know that many people otherwise would not get the justice they deserve. But so few solicitors gave this service, I was to learn. I spent days chasing false trails and when I did get through to somebody on this 'short list', every one of them said I needed someone who specialised in landlords and property. I knew this and had been misinformed about their abilities by others, otherwise of course I wouldn't have wasted my time, or theirs.

Patrick, my first husband, said I could use his solicitor (and generously offered to pay) if I couldn't find anyone. I was tempted, but as I'd been told that it could be a long and protracted case, it was really out of the question. There would be someone out there but I needed some time to clear my head before I set out to find him.

Other things more pressing were demanding my attention. Susie's marriage was going through a rocky patch and I was spending a lot of time with her. She had met Gerry, fourteen years her senior, whilst still at the Ballet School. From her early days at the junior school, through to the upper school, she had shown outstanding talent. We were told that there was every chance she would become a (world famous) prima ballerina. Unfortunately, Susie became obsessed with her weight – as many dancers do – and decided that 7st 4lbs was far too heavy for a swan. And even six stones was. When she got down to a 'comfortable' five and a half stones, her boyfriend of the day threatened to leave her if she didn't put on weight. Incredibly, it had the desired effect (anyone who has ever had dealings with victims of anorexia nervosa will know that no amount of tears, cajolery or threats will work, usually). Susie did put weight back on and for a while she was happy. Almost inevitably, however, she went back on her rigid diet of phantom food as I called it (she would pretend to have 'just eaten' whenever we saw her). Again, miraculously, she managed to come to her senses.

The Ballet Company hierarchy, rather than giving support to their highly talented pupil, distanced itself from her problems, created to a great extent by the rigorous and demanding standards, the obsession with honing bodies into fat free zones.

It was during this unsettling phase that Susie met Gerry. He worked in the city in those days (another one) and she was smitten instantly. They married shortly afterwards and set up home together at Gerry's bijou des. res. in Chelsea. Six years later, the union was falling apart. Naturally there were lots of tears, much soul searching and plenty of smashed crockery. They eventually split up and finally divorced.

Susie needed to work – not from a financial aspect as Gerry's settlement was enough to set her up for the rest of her life – but the life of leisure and luxury had begin to pall long before things started to go wrong. After all, most of her life prior to her marriage had been spent in a disciplined environment, where hard work was de rigeur. A respite from it is one thing, but something so deeply ingrained was always likely to surface. She couldn't go back to dancing as she was out of shape (NOT fat Susie, heaven forbid) but rather out of practice and too old at twenty-six.

She had a good singing voice (and looked gorgeous) so I introduced her to Mac, a musician acquaintance who had his own small studio. They worked together on a few ideas for several months, but nothing came of it. During this time they had started a relationship and eventually married in Las Vegas (Laura the bridesmaid, 'Elvis Presley' the best man). They bought a mews house in Camden before settling in Mill Hill, north London.

Kieran rang to say that he would like to come and live at my flat. I hadn't spoken to him for months and he had the nerve to propose this life-changing plan. Even to expect me merely to speak to him was ambitious, but this was a sectionable offence (if Guy had still been around, I would have told him to get over here quick as there was a suitable case for treatment coming round). I was so taken aback that I said we'd discuss it – although the answer was no.

He arrived that evening with a van full of furniture – just in case I said yes. And if I didn't, could he store it anyway as the house he'd been living in was now sold. He rented a barn in a field near Potters Bar to store some of his cars but as it was open-sided he didn't want to expose his stuff to the elements. There was also a donkey in the same barn.

I reluctantly agreed to store some of the furniture, but not Kieran. After the initial shock, I had vaguely toyed with the idea that it might be a good thing if he did move in as it would make the landlords back off possibly. However, as I wasn't allowed to take in lodgers – and I didn't want to flaunt the terms of the lease – I knew that from a financial point of view it would cost me money if he were not to pay rent. Money I didn't have. He said that he would do all the little jobs and repairs around the place, but how often does one's Hoover break down? And I'd been taught how to change a fuse over dinner at that Match Making evening. Also, we wouldn't last five minutes together in that close situation. He had a very persuasive and winning manner, admittedly, but the clincher came when he said that he might want to bring one or two of his cars and work on them from time to time in the private forecourt area. "I'm sure the landlords won't mind if I occasionally have a car up on a small pile of bricks."

I knew that he was winding me up. But then again, who knows?

His refectory table fitted into my large hall but where was my small oak one (a replacement for the beloved Art Deco that had just had to go to pay off some debts) going? He said that he would store it in the shed. I realised that it was rubbish; nevertheless I said it could only be stored on condition that it wasn't ruined and if it were, I would keep his in exchange.

He agreed (of course he would agree to anything at that stage as he assumed he would win me round in the likely event). I took his huge desk, a couple of chairs, three towel rails (unused, I should imagine), and various sundry items. I turned away the fridge (had it been full, I might have kept it), a vast settee and a nest of tables. I was not sure, either, about the bags full of clothes, as I didn't want my flat to be used as a dressing room. He reassured me that he'd kept one set back for 'business', the rest were on him. As a token of goodwill, he'd brought me a bag of apples. I said I'd rather the donkey have them, then it might leave my table alone.

He knew of course that I was short of money and selling my home from under my feet, so he offered to buy my 18th century square piano. A rare antique like that should have been sold years ago, I can hear Dan's solicitor cry. However, it wasn't that simple.

Many years before I met Dan, I'd gone to Phillips Auctioneers on one of the rare occasions when I did visit these places, as someone had asked me to look out for old sheet music for them. I was successful and bought a pile, including one that I kept myself as the cover was so kitsch. Black and white design of a stylised thirties couple in a field of flowers entitled *Knee Deep In Daisies And Head Over Heels In Love With You*. If only I'd been able to afford Arthur Askey's little white piano that was also on offer that day, they would have complemented each other perfectly.

I did buy a piano of sorts that day, the 18th century one Kieran now wanted to buy. Made by the esteemed master craftsman Clementi, the case was beautifully decorated with trailing garlands of roses and honeysuckle. Unfortunately, it *was* only a case, all the strings were missing, but it was only twenty pounds and so very beautiful. I did think that one day someone might lovingly restore it (that would have cost a great deal of money, hundreds if not thousands of pounds). Meanwhile, it would be extremely decorative despite the 'dummy' keyboard. This keyboard was to come in very useful one night, however, saving what could have otherwise turned into a rather ugly scene.

My mother was visiting and I had some musician friends round one evening – she loved meeting them but had to write their names down afterwards as she hadn't a clue about anyone, "I must tell Jean, she'll know who he was."

"He's still alive, Mother. I know he didn't look it…"

This particular night, one of the founder members of the Sex Pistols, Glen Matlock, had popped in and was playing *Pretty Vacant* on my grand piano – although originally, he was the Pistols' bass player. No one was paying much attention to him, as the funny cigarettes had taken hold by now; that is, apart from my mother who was standing over him, arms folded and clucking disapprovingly. Finally she couldn't stand it any longer and said, "You've got a *lovely* face, but you can't play. Let me show you."

She elbowed him out of the way and started playing her favourite hymn, *Surely Goodness and Mercy* at a speed the Sex Pistols would have approved of. She went off to make tea and 'sit quietly for a bit', but came back around midnight to chastise Glen once again. In the voice she normally used on 'thugs and creeps', she laid down the law, "Stop it *now*. It's far too late to be playing that stuff." Glen meekly slunk into the other room ('sorry missus') and bashed away happily on the dummy keyboard until breakfast was served (wine and sausage sandwiches) three hours later.

I wondered why Kieran wanted my historic piano case when he was trying to offload his own furniture.

"To help you."

"How much will you give me for it?"

"Fifty pounds."

"Fifty pounds? No way."

"Eighty then."

"OK, but I suppose you're going to sell it and make a fortune."

"I wouldn't do that."

My withering look made him laugh.

"I might have someone who wants it. I've told them about it."

"You are so outrageous. Go on, take it, I need the money."

My mother sent me the odd ten pounds now and again, but she had very little herself and lived as frugally as I did. She always said that it was to cover costs when she stayed but really I felt so dreadful taking anything. It made her feel that she was helping me, so I had to. I tried not to let my daughters know how bad things really were as neither Laura nor Rebecca were in a position to help.

For the most part, the girls thought my depression was due to missing Dan and to the problems I was having at the flat. Indeed, these were the main problems as money is of little interest to me usually, but it had become increasingly problematic now that I couldn't support myself on even a modest scale. Money also is empowering and I need to feel strong in my ongoing battle – even knowing that I had the next quarter's rent in the bank rather than worrying that the all-important deadline might not be met, would have taken off a lot of the pressure. I also would have liked to have been able to take a taxi to Portobello Road as standing in an empty road at 5.30 a.m. with heavy bags full of stock on a dark winter's morning is a bit frightening. I know that my stock is worthless, but a potential mugger doesn't know that. Odd people do walk by and I feel extremely nervous – especially if I miss the bus and have to wait a long time for the next one. The few times when I have been forced to hail a cab (I have a ten minute walk at the other end and extra heavy stock is simply not a walking matter), after expenses I have been lucky to come home with any profit at all.

Kieran's money went on bills and car boot treasures. I was thrilled to pick up an Art Deco rug (for £3), which would cover a large cigarette burn left by a short-sighted guest (although how anyone except Salvador Dali could mistake a soft expanse of pink Wilton for an ashtray is a mystery). Happily, the rug blends in perfectly and I'm almost tempted to ring my ex-friend and invite him back to repeat his anti-social habit on the curtains as I've seen some great, but very expensive thirties material in an antiques shop.

Prior to my current predilection for all things geometric, I had a love affair with the flowing Art Nouveau period – swirly lamps, organically inspired furniture and pre-Raphaelite maidens – and then a brief flirtation with Pembroke tables and Georgian windows. In fact, Georgian houses are still my idea of the definitive house; the purity of line and perfect proportions are unsurpassable. However, I didn't always have such good taste.

When I was first married, Patrick and I lived in a flat in north London (underneath Jeffrey Bernard actually, who looked incredibly well then, very handsome, like Elvis Presley). Patrick was interested in Roman history and so naturally we spent our honeymoon in Rome. We proudly displayed the souvenirs on our formica hatch flap when we returned. One day I covered one wall of our sitting room in paper patterned with Roman busts and axe heads. It toned beautifully with the grey flecked carpet and eight-seater blue studio couch. In hindsight it looked like a mini-cab waiting room but at the time it seemed to us as chic as an apartment on the Via Veneto.

Inspired by my handiwork, I papered almost the whole of our first house in Muswell Hill. The hall was tiny to start with and the red flock reduced it to Lilliputian proportions. The dining room in thick embossed gold leaf was a dead ringer for the wrapper room at Terry's chocolate factory. The children had nightmares after I papered their bedrooms with images of Victorian dolls, stern and menacing (I drew smiles on each one in the end). I left the sitting room au naturel, partly because we hardly ever went in there as it was furnished with the odd hand-me-down chaise longue, Victorian prints and a Davenport from my in-laws (not our taste at all). Eventually, this simplistic, uncluttered theme got to me and the Terry's All Gold, curry house flock and creepy dolls were buried under several coats of white emulsion.

Good taste is of course arbitrary. We all think our own taste is best (although surely no one seriously thinks that shell suits and serrated paper cocktail mats are a good thing). I know that if I bought only the sort of things I liked for the stall, I would sell very little. Some of the ghastly things people buy to actually wear astound me. I have heard myself agreeing with their fulsome praise, "Yes, it is an incredible brooch." I always had my fingers crossed behind my back and it was sort of true as I really meant yes, it was an incredible brooch in that it was so incredibly horrible). Nevertheless I thought *'liar'*, don't say a word, let people make up their own minds. So in the main I wasn't any good at selling as it went against the grain to sell what I perceived as bad taste.

When my mother was younger, she worked in a store in Bradford called Busby's – now long gone. Run by a Quaker family, it was a popular place as the prices reflected the altruistic nature behind the enterprise. However, my mother took the altruism that bit too far as she was frequently heard telling customers not to buy something if the colour clashed with her hair, say, or her bum didn't look big *enough* in it.

"It makes you look flat, it's not nice, you want something that will show off your curves."

One of the directors eventually took her to one side and said, "Dorothy, I know you're being honest and I wouldn't want you to be anything else, but occasionally people have taste that you may not agree with, and they may actually like a pink coat with red hair." Apparently my mother's indignant reply was, "Well, what are they doing in a lovely shop like this, then?"

# CHAPTER THIRTEEN

Contrary to popular belief, Bradford is not just a city of mass murderers, Asian riots and derelict satanic mills, it is also the home of the largest photographic museum in Europe, the best fish and chips in the world and an eclectic mix of sons and daughters such as Sir Frederick Delius, J. B. Priestley, Sir Edward Appleton, Ade Emondson, Albert Pierrepoint (the last hangman), Tony Richardson, Billie Whitelaw and David Hockney to name but a few. I thought the long checklist merited a book and I approached the Bradford library as I learned they would sometimes publish books such as this. The chap I saw was very enthusiastic but said that as the budget for the year had been spent, it would be at least eight months before it could even be considered. I waited patiently – I had no alternative, no major publisher was going to be interested in such a parochial idea. When I hadn't heard anything after ten months I rang to see what was happening, only to be told that the chap I'd seen had now left and new ideas would have to be put on hold for a year as there were other plans in the pipeline. A friend touted it around as a radio idea (other major cities would be included as part of the appeal), but it was at the time of cutbacks so it ran out of steam.

I have never lost my enthusiasm for Bradford though (apart from when I first left as a teenager aching to escape my provincial roots) and whenever I visit, I always go to Salts Mill as it is home to the world's biggest collection of art by David Hockney.

Textile magnate Sir Titus Salt built the huge mill and its surrounding model village in the mid nineteenth century and it is preserved in its entirety as a testament to this great visionary, thanks to another, twentieth century visionary, the late Jonathan Silver. Unlike Salt, Silver did not build almshouses or schools, but he did make astonishing things happen. In collaboration with David Hockney, he opened the 1853 gallery in 1987 which in turn attracted business and commercial ventures such as Pace Micro Technology plc – Britain's pioneering company in digital technology for satellite receiving equipment – thus consolidating his regeneration of the mill. A lover of the arts, Silver created a space for theatrical events, attracting such luminaries as Alan Bennett and raising thousands of pounds for local charities.

The mix of these and other new ventures has brought capital investment, jobs, new housing as well as millions of tourists from all over the world. Salt could so easily have become Silver, but he was not into self –aggrandisement. Sir Titus Salt was also his hero, so there was no question of changing the name.

I met Jonathan on several occasions as he was either buzzing about in the gallery or having informal meetings in the Diner – the airy, exotic restaurant adjacent to the up-market Home section run by brother Robin and his wife Pat (who now run Salts in its entirety). Unassuming in both dress and manner, it was hard to believe that he controlled this burgeoning empire. When my mother first saw him she was aghast, "He looks like a scruff, I can't believe it. And David's (Hockney) family's so nice.

Come again Mother?

She did get to like him very much once she had got used to his appearance and the more she heard about his philanthropic deeds.

I was invited to the opening of an exhibition of new drawings by David Hockney in the new gallery as the 1853 gallery was filled to capacity (not only are the walls lined with works of art but the floor space offers up a varied attraction of the unusual and lush – old looms stand juxtaposed alongside banqueting tables filled with books and enormous vases of fresh lilies). I decided to go even though I was still feeling very anti-social, preferring to shut myself away in my dungeon each night – at least it was peaceful once the workmen had gone. My mother, I knew, would love to go, as she would know many of the people who would also be invited – 'thugs and creeps' – only joking, I think. It wasn't for a few weeks anyway, so by then I might really look forward to it. However, there was to be a dramatic change in events, resulting in Laura's name being added to the guest list.

Terrifying earthquakes had hit Los Angeles and Laura was caught up in the thick of them. For two weeks she had slept (slept being the operative word) with her escape bag at the ready and fully dressed, uncomfortable mountain boots and all. Her house constantly shook and cracks and fissures appeared. She came out of it unhurt, but her only thought was to come home. She'd been feeling homesick for some time and the daily grind was soul destroying not to mention physically wearying. She had many great memories of her time there but her main objective had not been achieved, so this was the clincher.

Patrick rented a house for Laura in Fulham and a couple of her friends moved in to help with expenses. She signed with a new agent and soon settled back into London life.

We decided to have a holiday together incorporating the Hockney party and staying a few days with my mother. We caught a coach to Bradford – big mistake – it took seven hours as it went to places like Sheffield on the way. There used to be a coach that went from Bradford to Darjeeling apparently (so Bhim said). If it worked on the same principle as the one we got, anyone over fifty would be met by an undertaker at the final destination. Laura said she would like to hire a car once we got to Bradford as we were going to spend some time in the Lake District, visit Arnside to see if my 'giraffe' trees were still there. As she only had an American driving licence, she had to get an automatic – which didn't bother me as my only concern was that she would remember to drive on the left. I was quite nervous but if I'd known that *she* was terrified then I would never have agreed to hire a car. The little lanes and twisting roads were not something she was used to and she only relaxed once we hit the motorway.

Over the years I've gone back several times to Arnside as it's not only nostalgic but also it's one of those places where nothing much has changed; even the smells are the same. Usually, childhood haunts appear smaller in adulthood but with Arnside it's the other way round. The Knott is vast, not the small hillock I remember and it's a miracle I only got lost the once. The ossified giraffes – admittedly resembling silver birch trees a little more now – still cling on for dear life and that stunning view is more breathtaking with each visit.

The estuary is not a safe place to swim as there are notorious quicksands but when the tide is out there is one safe route across to Grange on the other side. Many years ago Prince Philip was taken across by the only man left who knew the precise path. (I think the sands of *time* got him in the end). One summer we had a great week when the caretaker of the private boys' school bordering on the estuary let us use the swimming pool as the boys were at home for the holidays. Rebecca learned to swim in there, I do believe.

Laura and I went to look at the estate my father had managed. Mainly woods, it stretched for miles along the beach to Silverdale. The owner at the time lived on the edge of the estuary in an imposing house with Ionic columns. Sadly, the house is now broken up into flats. We had lived there for the first year until we moved into the lodge and my main memory was of the family's lovely golden retriever, which followed me everywhere, and how desperate I was to keep it when we moved back to Bradford two years later. To compensate, my parents had bought me a frisky terrier which did eventually win my heart – so much so that I used to sneak him into bed with me. However, Laddie, as I named him, used to jump over the gate and chase the chickens in the allotment opposite. My father kept raising the gate until at ten foot, he said that was it, Laddie would have to go. I could not believe that my parents could be so cruel, especially as I used to see him from the bus sometimes, playing in his new street with his new best friend. It affected me deeply and to this day I'm not keen on animals (don't get close or they'll be taken away syndrome) and I *hate* bloody chickens.

We stopped next at the Redwell Inn in Arkholme as it was owned by comedian Jim Bowen. As it was residential, we decided to stay the night. Both Jim and his wife were very welcoming and we had a great evening as his regular jazz band (he plays trumpet with them) was playing that night. I'm not actually a jazz fan any more but in that setting and impromptu (to us) we enjoyed it.

I bought some cheap bits of jewellery at our next stop, Carnforth. I was particularly pleased with a marcasite watch that I picked up for a few pounds as when I cleaned it I discovered it was silver and worth at least eighty pounds. Laura bought an enormous mid-nineteenth century bible with brass bindings, which will go with all the other religious artefacts that she has around her place. She isn't overly religious but she does like her crosses. She even put two up in the room we shared at Jim Bowen's until I threatened to leave and, as I had the money for the trip, she had no choice but to take them down.

The weather was glorious and we were sorry when it was time to head back to Bradford. As we dropped off the hired car, I noticed something glistening on the roof. It was the watch. We had driven with it perched up there for three days along twisty roads. I must have absent mindedly put it there when I was sorting things out, although I can't remember doing it. Amazing that it hadn't fallen off before the sun had welded it to the roof.

The weather held for the party, so we were able to wear nice floaty, summery things. As I predicted, my mother knew many of the other guests and was in her element as Laura would and did say. We didn't know anyone apart from the now late Richard Whiteley who had lived near my mother at one time.

He joined our table and kept us entertained for most of the evening, as away from his *Countdown* persona, he was quick witted and funny. I sat next to a sculptor from Sheffield who was interesting enough but I obviously confounded him as he said at one point, "Thar mother's alreet and thar daughter's alreet, but I'm not so sure about thee." He decided by the end of the evening that I was 'alreet' after all and said he would like to see me again. Sadly, I couldn't have coped with the accent.

I went to have a chat with David Hockney (I might pick up the odd quote for future use) and I had known him vaguely from my student days but certainly hadn't had contact for years. However, my mother didn't give that a second thought as she made a beeline for him first, "Hello David, you remember our Lily." (Statement, not question).

"No."

"Yes you do," she insisted. "You know, the Students Jazz Club."

He didn't. He looked panicky as he backed up against a portrait of a naked youth.

My mother was staggered, "David, you DO!" she admonished firmly.

Time to come to his rescue. "Don't worry, *I* hardly remember me from my student days. I'll settle for a personal guided tour of your collection – for old times sake of course."

I don't remember how the evening ended but according to my mother I was disgusting and according to Laura I was hilarious. Apparently I climbed over high railings into a children's playground (this in the dark sometime after midnight) and had a go on everything. We had to walk into Shipley from Salts (fifteen minutes or so) and I staggered down the middle of the road until my daughter dragged me back. I sat in the gutter a few times (tiring work swinging – or should that be *swigging*?) My poor mother was really upset and cried, I gather.

I won't go out ever again. That's obviously the answer. I can't trust myself to only have a couple of glasses of wine any more. I don't know why, but I feel so agitated when I'm in that kind of environment now and the only way to cope is to have a few drinks. Then I can't stop, the one for the road becomes one for every autobahn in Europe.

Despite being drunk in charge of a playground and upsetting my mother, I enjoyed the break with Laura and dreaded getting back to 'reality'. I was nervous every day about opening the mail, but what was going to greet me now after five days away, I wondered?

A telephone bill. I can cope with that, well I can't pay it, but at least it's not life threatening. An estate agent's letter informing me how desirable my flat is and would I consider selling it as people were queuing up. A statement that I'd won fifty thousand pounds (I still don't understand how a company get away with putting this in writing and then give you a novelty key ring instead). There was a letter from the landlords (I'd to brace myself to open this one) informing me that the water would be turned off for four hours whilst maintenance work was carried out. As mine had virtually been off for months, I wasn't impressed. It's interesting that the landlords are very conscientious about trivia like that, but when it comes to informing me about major building works to be carried out just outside my flat they are very remiss. I haven't had one letter about these events (let alone an apology), but lots of letters informing me that major works were to be carried out *in* my flat.

The only other envelope looked intriguing rather than frightening, as it wasn't from any recognisable source. Inside was my Decree Absolute. I felt nothing. Just deflated. What an anti-climax. I thought I'd at least sob my heart out and run up another huge telephone bill.

It looked like getting my name off the Hastings property was proving difficult – I'm still not sure to this day why it took another four years from the Decree Absolute coming through before it was resolved. All I do know is that there was a recession and the house on which we'd taken out a second mortgage had now decreased in value by around fifty thousand pounds. If Dan couldn't meet the debt – and he wasn't earning much at the time, apparently (despite touring extensively abroad), then I would be liable. I was damned if I was going to pay for Dan to live with his girlfriend in what was once *my* home. I wasn't allowed back in (the locks had been changed just in case), although it was technically still half mine.

Dominic was partly to blame for the delay as he was spending less time in the office. He was becoming disenchanted with his day job and was talking about packing it in and going off to America. He still had his sense of humour, but that was turning blacker. He sent me a copy of a letter that he'd received from a victim of crime support group after he'd reported that someone (a client, I believe) had threatened to silence him for ever. (I *told* him not to sing *The Times They Are A'Changin'* to potential bankrupts). The letter read as follows:

"We were very sorry to hear from Marylebone Police that you were recently a victim of a threat to kill." It then offered its services in other languages if necessary and apologised for not being able to replace stolen money. It ended with, "We do hope you will be OK, but you can always call us if you need to even if, by then, it is some time after the event. Yours sincerely, Alan."

Dominic had scribbled on the bottom after highlighting the last sentence, "Would this be a little too late Al?"

One day I rang his office to be told that he hadn't been in for two weeks. I called his flat on and off but there was no reply. I desperately needed to talk to him about the house situation but he was simply not returning messages to anyone. It transpired that he'd locked himself in his place with all his clients' files (the few clients he had left) and wouldn't come out or speak even, despite neighbours and friends shouting through the letterbox. Eventually the police broke in and the files were returned. Dominic went away for a while to sort his head out and came back as upbeat as ever – if a tad religious.

There had been a two week respite from the works in the adjacent rooms – if I'd only been told, I could have relaxed instead of being on tenterhooks wondering when the crashing and smashing would start up – but the men were back with a vengeance. Ladders and planks of wood were blocking the corridor. The only way through would be to crawl under or vault over the top. I shouted for help and a chap in a suit came out of one of the rooms. A mobile phone clamped to his ear, he finished his conversation before saying to me, "Sorry, my man's just gone out, he'll be back in a minute." He then returned to the storeroom-cum-flat and shut the door. I was left standing there for at least five minutes before normal service was resumed.

When I returned, I wrote one of my regular missives to the management and enclosed damning photographs (I always took a camera out with me now). I said that I wasn't prepared to pay service charges in the light of recent events. I had fought for a reduction in the service charges in the past, as I simply wasn't getting anything but the most cursory service. Even my bin bags were left to pile up for days outside my door instead of the scheduled daily removal and I have one photo showing eight days worth, all carefully dated via headlines from the day's newspaper. The communal corridors and entrance halls in the rest of the building were cleaned every day but my area was a no-go zone. I was so ashamed of the contrast between the stage-managed opulence of 'front of house' and the stark difference once through the connecting door to my part. Incidentally, the front of this door, on the swish side, was beautifully painted in a dark mahogany shade, with a gleaming solid brass knob, whilst on the side facing my corridor it was covered in deep scratches and was filthy and knobless. (I sometimes think that's how I would like to see the landlords' gofer).

I received a letter by return agreeing to a fifty per cent reduction for a quarter, although no apology for the inconvenience and suffering that these works were inflicting, just a lot of waffle about cleaning contractors and external contractors. The service charge reduction, however, wasn't the 'gesture of goodwill'purported but rather a cheap cover with which to broach the buy-out issue again.

I did meet the company's broker shortly afterwards, but

I had no problem in turning down the new but equally risible offer.

Now that I had turned the second offer down, I was very apprehensive again, wondering what new tactics would be deployed. My sleeping patterns were erratic and I was having regular panic attacks. I didn't want to go on anti-depressants – and my doctor was not keen to administer them generally anyway. Some doctors believe a course of tablets can sustain one through a bad patch and when the time is right, dispense with them without ill effect. I'm too much of an addictive personality to risk such treatment (even though I have been told that certain anti-depressants are not addictive). I would probably end up bingeing on drugs and alcohol, hitting rock bottom in a filthy cockroach-infested hovel. At least I'd be home then.

In the end I agreed to see yet another counsellor but again I cancelled the course after just two sessions, as he wanted to find the answer in my childhood. Even those two hours had engendered a mild (but intensifying) resentment against my mother. In fact, I had a huge row with her as a result. She in turn rang my daughters as she was very upset and they each rang me then to say how much I'd upset Nana. I know I bloody have. And now I'm more depressed than ever.

My mother and I are always having rows as we are two very different people (and neither of us can accept it really) but they blow over very quickly. However, occasionally we do have these awful scenes when a lot of cruel and harsh things are said on my part. I regret them terribly afterwards and one day they will be the cross I have to carry, I know, but she is, I suppose, the one person in the world on whom I can vent my anger and frustration. It's so unjust, hurting the one you love.

I know that's what Dan and I did to each other – albeit by proxy. Dan had said that he didn't love me any more but I didn't believe him – maybe I didn't want to – but I was sure he still did. The girls had gone to see him without telling me, a year or so after we split up, and he told them that he would never again love anyone the way he had loved me. But then we all say things like that.

I do know that I never want to see Dan again as what we had was so passionate it can never be replaced by friendship. It has to be all or nothing.

# CHAPTER FOURTEEN

It was time to give my stock another airing in a new setting and Emma suggested that we try a mid-week fair at Towcester (or was it Telford?). Anyway, it didn't matter where it was; we never got to find out if anyone wanted our stock because we'd just finished unpacking when the heavens opened. It was so torrential – we were outside – that before we had time to cover things up, anything that could be ruined was. We sat in the car watching things disintegrate before our eyes. I lost over two hundred pounds worth (water colours had proved their authenticity and pulp fiction had earned its name). Emma reckoned her losses were about the same. Fortunately it had only cost us twenty pounds each for the stall (had it been Newark or Ardingly, we would have been sixty pounds down).

We'd arranged to stand next to another dealer friend, Adam Sankey, who had come over from France to do this and the fortnightly Kempton Park one. Fortunately, he'd had a good day at Kempton so he was mollified somewhat. Nevertheless he too lost a lot of stock. And this was the risk one ran at outside fairs.

On the other hand, on a lovely summer's day there is nothing nicer than stalling out amidst the rolling English countryside, chatting to friends or browsing around the rest of the fair (and with over two thousand stands at some of them, it can be a long and interesting task).

Adam had moved to a small village near Poitiers in France a couple of years before, and was loving every minute of it. He'd bought a house with a courtyard and terraced balcony that he was renovating himself. He'd recently discovered hundreds of bottles of wine hidden in the hillside wall of his garden. It was really good stuff and very drinkable (I can vouch for it as he gave us a dozen bottles each). He also found piles of beautiful new leather shoes from the nineteenth century, all in their original boxes and destined for an upmarket Chausseur in Paris. Obviously the house had once belonged to a master shoemaker (with a predilection for fine wine) and had stood empty all those years. Apparently, it's not unusual to come across derelict houses with items of furniture in situ. Some of these pieces can be of relative value but nobody bothers to steal them.

Adam had lived in his native Yorkshire for most of his life, apart from a few years when he lived in London. An actor and dancer, he had begun dealing, as many people do, to supplement an often irregular income. I first met Adam through Emma who had known him since they danced together in a show many years ago. We would meet up at Newark and the four of us (I was married to Dan at the time) would stay at the same B&B.

When Dan and I first broke up I went to stay with Adam a few times, as we would do fairs in the north together occasionally. Adam has the most wonderful and original sense of humour and being with him was a tonic. He lived in a tight-knit community and would pop into the local café run by a bunch of motherly souls who would fuss and see to his every need. He always threw a Christmas party for them at his place and one year as a joke he made up a strange concoction in the cat tray. The bemused quartet hesitated for only a second before tucking in. Adam did of course stop them but they would have eaten it as they thought the world of him.

His house looked like an ordinary late eighteenth century workman's cottage from the outside, but once inside it was another world. What had appeared small was in fact enormous. There were several rooms downstairs including the sitting room with a vast vaulted stone fireplace and a huge dining room complete with a Yorkshire range (very rare and valuable now). Upstairs a minstrels' gallery and three bedrooms, two with antique canopied beds. The bathroom had Edwardian fairground swing pulls for the light and lavatory flush and a 1920's drapers shop window dummy held the towels in her outstretched arms. And everywhere there was fascinating bric-a-brac and memorabilia, a veritable time warp.

Although Adam was in his fifties, he had only just learnt to drive so it was still something of a novelty to him (a white knuckle ride to me). We had planned to go to the Birmingham fair together (not that it was near to Adam but at least it was almost all motorway). We set off at 4.30 a.m. packed to the gills (Adam had big furniture that he wanted to sell and I had a couple of large, heavy bags). We broke down first about twelve miles from home. We called the AA from a nearby phone box (this was pre-mobiles being widely used so neither of us had one). About twenty minutes later a mechanic found us and after spraying something on the engine we were back on the road. Unfortunately, the same thing happened again and we went through a repeat performance ten miles further on. Of course we should have gone back but we'd spent a long time packing and we both needed to sell, so we talked ourselves into believing that it couldn't possibly happen again.

We were travelling alongside an enormous pantechnicon for what seemed like hours, as Adam couldn't pass it. I was listening to a riveting shipping forecast to take my mind off it when the car started to 'pink' again. What a nightmare, we had to get across into the slow lane but the bloody lorry was in the way and cars were hooting as we started to slow down. Adam couldn't find his hazard lights to let them know that we weren't just taking it easy. I think I was screaming at the Neolithic small town driver next to us to put his foot down like he would normally if we were in *front* of him. We did finally make it to the hard shoulder and Adam said he would go and find a 'phone.

I refused to be left at 5.30 in the morning in the pitch black with all those terrifying things hurtling by, so I went with him. We tossed a coin whether to go back or forwards (neither of us realised that arrows point the way), so we went forwards. Wrong. The 'phone was eight inches behind the car. At least we would be getting a new man this time. He didn't arrive for nearly three quarters of an hour, as he had to go down the motorway to come back up apparently. He said that he couldn't work on it on the motorway as the last time he did that he looked up to see a coach bearing down on him.

He towed us to Stoke on Trent where Adam was told that he would have to leave it, as the work couldn't be done that day. They got him a hire car back home and I was offered a lift in the pick-up truck to the station, to go back to London. I was given a tour around all the factories, "There's the Wedgwood kilns", as I had apparently missed the train and would have to wait for a couple of hours.

I had to stand all the way as this was the commuter train. When I arrived home I found that my bags had got squashed and two items of glass were broken and my last remaining gold bangle worth sixty pounds was now a piece of scrap worth twelve.

Birmingham was good, apparently.

The course at Whitegates had inspired me to have a go at writing again. I think Sam might have given it five out of ten for 'marked improvement'. Here are some of the lyrics:

## HE MUST HAVE SWALLOWED HIS SILVER SPOON

*Intro*
> He must have swallowed his silver spoon
> A long time ago
> For here he stands
> With nothing else
> But love to give me

*Verse*

> I don't need
> His old man's
> Second hand fortune

I can't use
Worn out shoes
Stepped in once too often
He must have swallowed his silver spoon
He must have swallowed his silver spoon.

My creative flash didn't end there. I wrote another, loosely based on Dan and me:

BREAKDOWN IN COMMUNICATION

*Verse*

When we've had a quarrel
Something's come between
I am in the desert
You're in Bethnal Green.

*Verse*

I feel like a prisoner
In the condemned cell
Solitary confinement
Is a living hell.

*Chorus*

We don't talk to each other any more
We don't say all the things we said before
There's been a breakdown in communication
Once we didn't need to say a word
Now the sound of silence can be heard
There's been a breakdown in communication.

And so on and so forth (at least Sam can't say 'Let's hear the rest of it then')

I called it a creative 'flash' because it went as quickly as it came. Rather than recruit someone to make proper demos of these two half-decent songs, I listened to my own inept renditions and threw them in the bin. I'd tried, failed and now all I could see was my future, blank and on the edge of a permanent scream. Still, both Eastenders and Coronation Street were on television that night and I'd got cottage cheese with pineapple and a bottle of Poitier's finest red wine for dinner, so at least the future wouldn't kick in until tomorrow.

The girls had persuaded me to have some photographs taken as they thought I should do some advertising work – older models like Lauren Hutton and Issabella Rosselini were suddenly de rigeur – the pay was good and it would get me out of my regulation uniform (the cleaning-up clothes look). The photos duly arrived and they were horrible. My face looked as though it were made of pastry. Uncooked. If the camera never lies, then I really have lost everything. Susie thought it was hysterically funny. What a nasty girl. Just wait until she gets older – actually she's got one or two lines already. Laura arrived and wanted to know what the joke was. "The photos aren't that bad," she lied. "The make up was too heavy, that's all." That's all. I didn't have any lines until that make up went on, now they're here to stay. I didn't dare send the pics to anyone, even though I daresay I could have made a fortune out of Pancake – the batter mix, not the make up.

Around the time I'd had my creative flash, I also sent a synopsis of an idea I had for a book about women in rock, entitled (catchily, I thought), Frock 'n' Roll, to a literary agent. He had rung to say that there was a lot of interest, "And that's not Friday night agent bullshit."

It may or may not have been, but nothing was to come of it. I had written various rock profiles in the early eighties so fifteen years on, I thought it was about time for an update, but obviously nobody else did

Normally, a setback like this is just one of those things but when so much depends on a positive outcome, the rejection is proof that your talent, such as it may be, has gone along with everything else. It's not possible to see that this is how it has always been, that rejection is the nature of the beast. Everyone, no matter how great, has had to face rejection at some time or other (it took Brian Epstein a long time to persuade anyone to sign the Beatles and we all know the story of Van Gogh's posthumous fame coming a little too late to save him from a lifetime of angst). Nauseating self-pity takes over, followed by deep-rooted fear that your creative safety net has gone, leaving you out of kilter, lightweight and unstructured.

As an atheist I do not believe in divine intervention or God moving in mysterious ways, but it is interesting how something often does stop us in our miserable little tracks and kick-start us back into touch with the world. One such event happened to me recently and even though I would rather not have had the experience, nevertheless I am grateful for it.

It was a bitterly cold night and sitting huddled in a doorway in an affluent street in Marylebone was an old man, late seventies maybe, not begging but just sheltering from the insidious weather. I passed him by, then, consumed by guilt, I went back to a nearby café for a coffee and sandwich, which I then gave to him. He humbly thanked me and I was overcome at the sight of his gaunt grey face, so I found a policeman as the man was obviously desperately ill and wouldn't last the night in that doorway. The policeman immediately called for help and I left him gently comforting the pitiful poor old fellow who had crept quietly into a corner, not wanting to be a nuisance to anyone. How could his life have come to this, I wondered? I will never forget his defeated, tired face. And indeed, whenever I feel beaten I see it – as a reminder that I don't know the meaning of the word.

However, I am not all heart. I do get fed up with the 'Big Issue'. Don't get me wrong, I believe in the premise of course, and usually buy a copy, but I just wish I didn't have it thrust in my face fifty times a day, especially when I'm leaving the supermarket with a modest supply of rations. Despite my innocence (there are no luxury items in *my* shopping bag), I do feel incredibly guilty. That's the whole point, of course, a bit of conscience stirring. Perhaps I'm supposed to buy one from every seller. Some of the have-nots, however, do not endear themselves to us just-about-haves with their aggressive soliciting. Can of Special Brew in one hand, resentment in the other. These unsavoury individuals do not help the issue – big or otherwise. Although I did have a sneaking admiration for the bloke who used to stand outside of Selfridges in Oxford Street, his copies of the publication laid out in a neat arc on the pavement so that unencumbered, he could mock-gesture at the crowds whilst singing *Walk on By*. And most of them did.

I think a secret sign like the Freemasons' handshake should be devised, then rather than scurrying by, face averted, we could saunter past, confident that it would be correctly interpreted – that we were not all churlish bastards, but Big Issue friendly. I was so fed up with one individual who regularly blocked my path, waving his magazine threateningly an inch from my nose that I said to him on the last occasion, "No thank you, but I'll have a Gibbons Stamp Monthly if you've got one."

My fridge has packed up and I can't afford to buy another one, so it looks like I'm going to have to store Kieran's after all. It's actually quite a nice one as it's a giant Coca Cola can, but as it has no shelves, everything has to be stacked in a big pile. There won't be much in it though, so that really won't be a problem.

Kieran was thrilled to be able to help me out. And now that I had his fridge, he could raid it legitimately, he thought. Wrong. For every illicit swig of cooking sherry, there would be a bin liner of his clothes put out with the other rubbish-filled bags.

He sneaked in a revolting black plastic deckchair along with the fridge, insisting that it would tuck away neatly under the desk, but as the space was filled with his clothes, it didn't. He draped a tea towel over it, murmuring that I would learn to love it in time. Sensing my rising anger, he offered to take me out for a kebab. It did the trick. Such a rare offer was not to be argued over. Apart from the times he'd eaten with me, Kieran had consumed the same dish every night for the past two years, he said. But why a kebab?

"It's quick, nourishing – meat, salad, fruit, bread – and..." he paused for a second and then shouted, "DELICIOUS!"

I wish just for once though that Kieran could do something for me without wanting to spoil the nice gesture by making me lose my sense of humour (and boy, was he quick to point it out, "You're so bad tempered these days.") Call me a killjoy, but when a person takes you out to dinner to placate you for trying to squeeze a few more bits of junk into your already overcrowded flat, then he shouldn't expect to be able to bring in three large boxes of dog-eared filthy roadmaps on the back of that kebab and a half carafe of house wine.

And on the subject of kebabs, I do think Kieran should vary his diet perhaps, as he wouldn't let me go to the lavatory after him when we got back from the restaurant. "The smell is so bad, Dettol won't do, I'll have to brick it up."

That wasn't the only poisonous odour getting to me, as for months lorries would pull up outside my windows – sometimes as early as 6 a.m. – and leave the engines running until the back gates opened at 7 a.m. to let them in with their assorted building materials. The noxious fumes would seep in through my air vents despite repeated requests not to leave engines running. The noise of the lorries was bad enough (there was always a lot of pre-unloading activity) but the smell was extremely offensive and no doubt harmful. The management would write that the men had been told, but as the builders were constantly changing, the respite was never for more than a few days. To reiterate, by now, apart from myself and the head porter, no one else was living in this particular part of the building.

Paul, my doctor friend, had to go up north for a few days and as his partner (also Paul) was in America, he asked me if I would dog-sit for the weekend. I was happy to – anything for a change, and he was a good friend. I first met him through the other Paul, as we worked together on a music magazine. I was the editor at the time and Paul the art director. It was the early eighties and I was approached by the publisher as he knew that I had many contacts in the business. I ended up writing many of the features as we were on a very tight budget, so we couldn't afford to pay writers. It was great fun and lasted for almost a year before we ran out of money completely.

Over the years a close friendship had developed and now that I had parted from Dan, I saw even more of the two Pauls. My mother is terribly fond of them and they adore her. So much so that we have to spend Christmas with them, the party games just wouldn't be the same without my mother. They shriek with laughter at her. "You're so camp, Dorothy." (She never quite knows what they mean, but takes it as a compliment anyway). I think my mother likes the fact that they have been together for almost twenty years (more than many of her heterosexual friends have) and that they have 'a lovely home, gorgeous pink curtains and that soft shade of grey settee.' They also are genuinely interested in her Ripper et al stories (mind you, most people are).

I had nearly reached Paul's front door in Lewisham when I thought about my iron. I *had* turned it off. Had I? Yes of course I had. Had I though? I was sure I'd done that thing of saying aloud 'IRON OFF' with an accompanying chopping gesture (a bit like that Barbara Woodhouse 'sit' command to trainee dogs). So that was all right then.

"Paul, I think I've left my iron on, I'm going to have to go back, I can't stay all weekend if I'm worrying about it." He gave me the keys to the house as he would have left by the time I got back (two hours later). What a drag. I did this so often these days. It's all part of the stress thing.

It was dusk when I returned so I drew the curtains in every room as it was quite a big house and was overlooked, so I felt not only conspicuous, but also nervous. Paul said they'd never been burgled but neighbours had, and it would just be my luck if that night it were to be Paul's turn (so I turned on every light in the place as well). The main front curtains wouldn't close. I tugged and tugged but they were on one of those cords that mysteriously knots and will not budge. In the end, after this long wrestling match (the burglars no doubt on standby watching in wry amusement), I had to stick J-cloths all over the windows (two packs).

Stupidly, I didn't have Paul's number, so I had to wait for him to ring me. He didn't ring until 10 p.m. Meanwhile, I was desperate for a drink but the only wine I could find was the 'special' cache, rare fine wines coated in dust and cobwebs. I resisted for ages (the nearest off-licence was miles away), until in the end I thought, sod it, I couldn't face burglars without a glass of wine. I chose the cleanest bottle, assuming that was the cheapest, and settled down to what I hoped would be a peaceful night from now on. The dog wanted to go out in the back garden (it had been trained to foul the acacia border, away from soft furnishings), so I had no choice but to unlock the vast French windows – on and off – throughout the night (a small bladder problem, apparently). Paul was sorry when he phoned and told me to help myself to the good wine. At least that worked out all right.

Perhaps it was just as well that my father gave my beloved little dog away, as pets can be such a nuisance. Laura has four cats and they are fine until you step into the kitchen. Then they want to sit on your hands, if possible – hands that are trying to make a piece of toast for lunch. Cats don't even like toast but they know how much it annoys you if they pretend to. Years before, when the girls were little, we had two Siamese cats (bought in a weak moment for my little darlings who had begged and cajoled for pets for ages). They were actually adorable as kittens, but not quite so appealing (to me) in bony adulthood. The children christened them Rover and Fido because of their peculiar canine-like growl. We spent hours trying to teach them to miaow, but sadly, only the angelfish caught on. When the girls moved into their own places, Laura won the fierce battle over custody and for the first time in twelve years, I could leave food exposed without fear of it ending up in a cat or under the bed – or worse.

I once had a dinner party and unwisely left the cooked (and therefore very hot) chicken pieces wrapped in bacon out on the oven top for a moment whilst I refilled glasses. Rebecca was about four at the time and she came into the sitting room and asked me in an extraordinarily loud voice if it was 'alright if the cats were playing with the chicken'. Everyone froze. I rushed into the kitchen to find the cats patting hot chicken pieces around, for all the world looking like they were playing a feline version of lacrosse, their little cupped paws serving as rackets. I quickly scooped up the chicken pieces, ran them under the hot tap and calmly announced that everything was fine and dinner was now ready. All the guests said the food was delicious – and that's the nice thing about friends, they're prepared to lie to spare your feelings.

# CHAPTER FIFTEEN

It was just as well I had a loaded camera at the ready because I certainly needed it when I returned from my weekend at Paul's. There was an open Stanley knife, an unattended, plugged in electric drill, cables snaking along the corridor – all right outside of my door. Had I been coming out of my flat instead of going into it on this Monday morning, I would have trodden on the open knife and loose nails. The foreman apologised and quickly moved things, but of course nothing should have been there in the first place. I got some very graphic and horrifying photos. My case was getting stronger all the time.

I never speak to the management team if I can help it, but particularly the main man, as he often can't be bothered to answer my letters and when he does, he deftly evades many of the main points. He is a short but arrogant man and I cannot bear even having to discuss relatively normal things with him. I am not the only one who has this opinion in my block. Many's the time at rent officer meetings, other tenants have accused him of rudeness and arrogance. However, when he wants something from the tenants, he can then be quite oleaginous. (I hope I never meet him in the corridor in this mode because if the slippy floor doesn't get me, the oil slick will).

New gates have been fitted outside of my sitting room – only a few feet away from my window so now I have a regular clanging as they open and close, on and off all day long until late into the evening. Drivers are impatient and frequently hoot their horns for the porters to open them few people can be bothered to get out of their cars to press the buzzer that alerts the porter to their presence. The pedestrians' gate is also part of this set-up and that clangs loudly each time it shuts. The electrical unit controlling them has been fixed to the white tiles barely a few inches away from my sitting room window. The tiles surrounding it have all been smashed and just left. I wouldn't put it past somebody to have worked out that it might be a good idea to give me round the clock noise pollution as that might finally drive me out. It's strange how I can listen to rock music so loud that I'm partially deaf for a while afterwards and not mind at all, but the minute a car hoots its horn, followed by a double clang (the gate reverberates) and a loud clunk, *this* percussive sound makes me want to kill. I can't even sit in the relatively quiet bedroom as apart from its own furniture, all of Kieran's stuff is there and I'm damned if I'm going to perch on top of his desk every night.

My mother rang to say that she has been diagnosed as having Glaucoma. It's a serious problem that can lead to blindness if not kept in check, so it means she will have to take tablets every day for the rest of her life. It can also be hereditary, so I will have to keep a look out for warning signs such as haloes round electric lights.

"Oh, I don't see things like that," said my mother dismissively. "No, I see sputniks."

That's called madness, Mother, not glaucoma.

My answer phone is not exactly full of exciting messages these days, so I was pleasantly surprised to receive one from an old friend, Jonathan Landers, hinting that there might be some good news at last about a television series that we had devised sometime ago.

I first came up with the basic idea when I was working in radio in the early eighties. As most of my regular team had now left, I had to take it to another department which I occasionally worked for. However, I knew and liked Marsha Brendon (my would-be saviour in the editing room at Talk Radio). We did a pilot together and I gave it to the head of the department. He liked it and suggested that I did the research and one of his teams would present it. I was pretty cheesed off as it *was* my idea and I *was* a presenter in my own right. He scheduled the series to go out at 2 a.m. – the graveyard shift. Only dozing night watchmen and hacked off cab drivers would hear it. Both Marsha and I were convinced that it was prime time material, as indeed were those who took part; people like Spike Milligan.

I called it *Heroes Heroes*, the idea being that even celebrities have their heroes, people they would love to meet. The format was simple; celebrity in studio with his or her hero, chatting informally together. The celebrity as interviewer, in other words. It would of course be unscripted and as it would be pre-recorded any 'lulls' would be edited out.

I reluctantly went along with this missed opportunity, dreading having to tell the willing participants that it was part of insomniacs programming.

Jonathan agreed that it was wasted but said that in a way it was fortuitous as he saw it as a television idea and suggested that we re-structure it with that in mind. His brother is a respected Hollywood agent, so we sent it to him, as his contacts were greater than ours.

He liked it and said that he would put out feelers and get back to us.

Over the next two years he would raise our hopes. "Fox loves it, it's looking good. Jack Lemmon loves it, he wants in," all the while never losing his enthusiasm for the project (even though I did constantly) and until this day, obviously, is still trying to get it off the ground.

I called Jonathan back.

"It's looking very promising."

"Don't you start, Jonathan, I've had enough of the false hopes."

"My brother has never given up on it you know, he really believes in it. Anyway, apparently there's renewed interest, so we might all get rich after all."

Wouldn't that be useful? I could get a new fridge.

In the meantime I couldn't live on pipe dreams. I had

been down that road too often but it was nice to at least make contact with Jonathan again.

Meanwhile, reality bites. All the flats in the block are having video entry phones fitted so I'm getting one as well – this will be fantastic as I hate answering the door unless I know just who it is (even if the police bashed on the door I wouldn't let them in unless they knew the name of the court usher who 'had Peter Sutcliffe in once').

The workman had obviously only ever worked on a chain gang before getting the entry phone job, because he smashed big chunks out of my wall – newly decorated after the floods – in an attempt to attach it. Only after he'd gone did I see that the other side was also smashed, with a huge crack running from top to bottom.

The landlords said that someone would come by to check the damage and ascertain how big a job it was. Fifty men working flat out for six months might do the trick, I expect. No thanks. I couldn't even face the assessor, never mind further violation of my privacy, so when I was told that it would be a major job (the whole wall had to be re-built), I showed him the door. I've hung a few strategically placed pictures and some foliage and for now, that will have to do.

I never know what horrors to expect outside of my front door these days and today was no exception. A cockroach the size of a shoe. I'd seen Rentokil men hovering recently but I thought that was just a random swoop they might do every so often on the rat population. There was nothing in the shiny brochures currently in circulation about cockroaches. There was plenty about the elegant refurbishment and eminent people who had previously lived here, though. I scrawled on the bottom of one such brochure, "And even the humble basement can boast its royal connections, as the king of cockroaches has taken up residence as from this morning."

I often think of those halcyon days of parties and concerts, the fulfilling work, the happy home front and compare it to the harsh reality of now. I repeat, I've led a charmed life and it's certainly my turn for a bit of grief, but it's going on a bit too bloody long, I reckon. Just getting through a packet of condoms satisfactorily would do me for now.

I don't know why today's men make such a big meal out of using a condom (after all, they are two hundred times as thin as a crisp). Centuries ago in Constantinople, women shook the gritty sand from sea sponges and dipped them in lemon juice before inserting them vaginally – uncomfortable, but appropriate for winkles. In Victorian times, condoms were made of sheepskin – warm at least. Even legendary lover Casanova wasn't as selfish as he's been painted, as he not only wore protectors but he also made them himself by sewing fine strips of linen together, no doubt enhancing his reputation of always being in the sheets with someone.

Interestingly, the company that markets Durex, the world's leading brand of condom, also sells Marigold washing up gloves. And not many men want to wear those, either.

I do worry when I see young women hitting the bars and clubs as these days their capacity for drink seems as great, if not greater than their male counterparts. And we all know how invincible we feel after a night on the tiles. Anti-social diseases are the last things to think about in this sociable state, hence many women forget to pull rank when they've pulled Frank (or Dick) and can end up removing their underwear yet again, only this time for a clap doctor.

It's also a fact that drink can make one more, or less, tolerant. Intolerant simply means you go home alone. Tolerant means you go home with someone you wouldn't even spit on sober. I have never actually done the latter but I have woken up to find a good friend at my side. Neither of us could remember if we'd had sex or not as we were so drunk and we fervently hoped we hadn't (friends do not have sex) – and we probably hadn't as we were that paralytic, but the thought that we might have even tried was very nasty. And, predictably, it's there, uppermost, whenever we meet. We never mention it, but it's a barrier now so the friendship *has* suffered, even though we pretend that it hasn't.

As for the former, I have stormed out of many a situation in drunken high dudgeon. One can lose a lot of friends and lovers that way, and I have. Others simply ignore your excesses but give you a wide berth for a few days. One shameful incident has become folklore and the recipient, Graham, loves to recount it whenever possible. Graham had shown what he was made of that first lunch when he withstood Guy's blatant hostility. However, I would test him sorely a few months later.

His parents had a holiday flat in the south of France which Graham often used. He invited me along but forgot to tell me that two of 'the boys' (his drinking pals) were coming as well. Not only was it now not so cosy and romantic but also it was lop-sided – three men and me. It was a disparate set-up age wise, Andy (nineteen), George (fifty-eight), Graham (twenty-seven) and me (thirty-seven). Although that wasn't an issue normally, on holiday it could be. Andy would in all probability be chasing mademoiselles like a dog on heat, George wouldn't physically have the strength to do that, but he would be quick (and constant) with the smutty one-liners. Graham would naturally be distracted but unable to join in the fun and I would know that he would soon regret this foursome. He'd wish it were a threesome.

The flat was lovely, and at least the boys were staying in another part of the block, although they were meeting us for dinner at the local bistro. Graham had sung its praises ever since we planned the holiday so I was expecting something good.

The room was functional rather than interesting or snug and the tables were long benches for parties of eight or more. The bistro was famed for its mussels and that's what we had, a mountain of exquisite perfection. Unfortunately, neither Graham nor I got to eat ours because I took it into my head that Graham – who was sitting next to me – was talking about me to his buddies. We had been drinking practically all day so we were in very high spirits, but I 'turned'. I became the aggressive drunk. I stubbed my cigarette out in Graham's dinner (isn't that the pits?) and then flounced out of the restaurant. A couple of minutes or so later, Graham and Andy came out after me and found me doing handstands and cartwheels on the pavement. I refused to come back in and asked for the keys to the flat. I then went back on my own; up snickets and paths I had never seen before in my life and eventually, somehow, arrived back.

The next morning I woke early with that sinking feeling one has after such a night – a shameful awareness that something awful happened, but only hazy recollections. I crept out onto the balcony and waited for Graham to wake up and tell me that he was taking me to the airport.

All things considered, he was very nice about it, even saying that people often do excessive things on the first night but he did rub it in how much he'd been looking forward to the meal. I know, six weeks. I kept my distance that day but by the evening all was forgiven (to prove it, Graham even bought some condoms). To this day, I still think he was making up the handstands and cartwheels bit, but then again I am very good at them, after all, I was taught by professionals from Chipperfields Circus.

# CHAPTER SIXTEEN

I once wrote a feature on the growing trend of so-called antiques dealers who sell reproduction alongside the real thing. Many buyers simply can't tell the difference and unless the dealer is honest, they might go home with something that was made yesterday rather than yesteryear. Despite fairs organisers stipulating that these sorts of items must not be sold, many do nevertheless slip through the net.

I spotted a brooch on a stall at a fair this week and out of curiosity, I asked the price. The vendor told me it was Art Deco and had to be £150. Well I knew that it was a Butler and Wilson copy (they of course never purport that their goods are anything but either the real thing, or indeed a copy). Also, their goods are signed and they certainly weren't around in the thirties. Perhaps another customer wouldn't have the inside information or the knowledge to doubt the vendor – who probably was ignorant rather than crooked. Some go even further, labelling their goods, 'Lovely (you could almost get them on Trades Description alone with that), Victorian Toby Jug.' I grant you it might have come off Toby's market stall but that's where the ambiguity ends as I doubt it's over a few weeks old.

To the trained eye, copies are anathema and could never be mistaken for an original but newcomers to the trade and the innocent public are lambs to the slaughter and who, for some unfathomable reason, rarely complain should they ever discover the mistake. The silence of the lambs, I suppose.

A friend once made a refectory table. The top was made from wood washed ashore at Portland Bill and the base came from a huge Victorian desk. He 'aged' it over a six-week period, creating burn marks and staining it with ink, ox blood and urine – his own. Whenever people visited and needed to use the lavatory, it was only natural to direct them to the basement, "Please use the table on the left." When it finally went in a friend's shop window one Saturday night, there were three notes pushed through the door shortly afterwards with requests to view as soon as possible – all from respectable furniture dealers. As far as Gordon was concerned, he was a selling a table he had made. He had no intention of deceiving but he was interested in how well he had carried out the exercise. He didn't have to say anything as the dealers told him what the table was. Eighteenth century refectory, they all agreed; only one said it was a 'marriage' with the base being added perhaps fifty years later. When Gordon finally enlightened them, they were quite amazed and suitably embarrassed. Experts would have spotted the errors, but to an average dealer it was authentic. And of course the integral parts *were* 'antique', only the marrying and embellishments were new.

Before we married, Dan bought a reproduction gilt mirror for eighty pounds from one of the multi-stores (the other hundred or so looked just as 'old'). We relegated it to a spare room but then decided to put it in auction (I wanted to sell it at a car boot sale for a fiver) as we had bought a larger, early nineteenth century Gesso framed mirror for a hundred and eighty pounds – an absolute bargain. I warned Dan that his little mock Regency number wouldn't fetch much as it was only ten years old.

It fetched a hundred and sixty pounds. So not only had I blown all my credibility, but Dan then insisted that we buy our stock in future from John Lewis. (Only joking).

In the eighteenth century, a watchmaker called Christopher Pinchbeck invented a cheap gold substitute by fusing zinc and copper. This meant that the bourgeoisie could emulate the aristocracy at a fraction of the price. Today, genuine Pinchbeck is rare and can fetch as much as gold – a case of reproduction being meritorious in its own right. Some dealers will claim that every bit of brass or copper jewellery is

Pinchbeck and indeed it is now almost an accepted misnomer – although I still can't help snapping 'Rubbish!'

I suspect that most people today who knowingly buy reproduction antiques do so because they like the pristine. The scars of decades can be seen as ugly and disfiguring, whilst to others it is these very scars that make the item beautiful. I overheard a dealer sum it up neatly this week. A woman had been scrutinising a gold locket of his for at least five minutes and when she finally triumphantly proclaimed, "It's got a dent!" he swiftly replied, "Madam, you're probably half its age and you've got several."

Most dealers are honest and professional as they trade regularly in the same places but the few unscrupulous ones, not to mention the dilettantes, don't help the image. Every profession is infiltrated by types such as these but we do get a particularly bad press when anything untoward happens. I remember in particular when Ronnie Barker opened an antiques shop in the Cotswolds, he was accused of deliberately undervaluing an item that someone had brought in to him. Well for a start, that's the name of the game, paying less than something is maybe worth – otherwise we'd never be able to scrape a living, never mind make 'vast profits'. However, as Mr. Barker was not a specialist and a relative newcomer to the game (I believe he previously only knew a little about old postcards), he offered what he thought was a fair price, rightly or wrongly. Shamefully, the press went to town and smeared an innocent man, I believe. I know that I wouldn't have merited a front page spread if I'd made an offer someone COULD refuse.

If people are not sure about the authenticity of something, they should ask for a receipt with a description and estimated date. People really would think twice if they had to write 'Pinchbeck chain circa 2003'. However, we do get sick and tired of accusations that have no foundation from ill-informed members of the public whose only brush with antiques is as a viewer of related television programmes that can never really educate, as there are too many variables in this fascinating field. And unless one specialises, how can any broad based dealer be expected to know everything down to the last detail about every artefact that has been made over the last two or three hundred years? But again, to reiterate – that is no excuse for the people who trade under the generic antiques banner, yet sell modern gift shop bric-a-brac.

I was at a Sunday fair in a respectable south coast hotel and I might just as well have been in one of the seaside gift shops as, out of the forty or so stalls, only three were selling anything my grandmother might have vaguely recognised. I do not want to buy sugar false teeth and sickly smelling pot-pourri sachets in an antiques fair.

After my feature, a chap wrote in to say, 'In her collection of ceramic pug dogs, my wife has a most delightful biscuit barrel – it cost her just £6.75 a year or so ago in a Polperro gift shop; she loves it and would have paid much more. Indeed, we have seen it since in antiques shops, variously priced at £18, £35 and in the antiques department of a most prestigious store at £48 where she was told, "We believe it to be Victorian".'

It can't have been John Lewis's, that's for sure.

There are naturally many people who do not like antiques. Fake or reproduction antiques, indeed anything that reflects a bygone era. My mother is one of these – although she's not exactly at the cutting edge of modernity; rather bland but functional stuff. Neat would sum it up. Eau de nil shades with touches of lovatt green. I do have a problem with the 'knick knacks' dotted about though, as I truly hate them and my mother gets quite upset when I pour scorn on her 'exquisite' collection of china roses in small china bowls. She got her own back recently (not deliberately, I may say), when I was rhapsodising about a Victorian cherub that I'd just bought. It was made in such a way that it could sit on the edge of a table or shelf, its wings draped forward. It was painted in subtle flesh tones, the wings a soft golden yellow. She took one look, sniffed and said, "They (the wings) look like dead banana skins."

I think Peter Shaffer got the knick-knack aversion spot on in his play *Equus* when he wrote, 'All my wife has ever taken from the Mediterranean – from that whole intuitive culture – are four bottles of Chianti to make into lamps and two china condiment donkeys labelled Sally and Peppy.'

My mother's answer to that? "How common. Making lamps out of wine bottles."

*I* might just have to resort to making lamps out of Poitier's finest soon, as I sold my last decent one at a fair recently. I hadn't even thought about selling it as it wasn't worth very much but I couldn't have used it anyway if I didn't pay the outstanding electricity bill. The first lamp I sold after Dan and I split up was my favourite Art Nouveau stained glass one. A friend bought it to 'keep it in the family'. As she's a good deal older than I, she reckoned that way I'd get it back some day.

I wish she hadn't said that. I can't bear to think about my friends not being around any more – assuming some won't be. Harold Pinter apparently worries so much about his older friends and acquaintances that he has started to miss them already.

# CHAPTER SEVENTEEN

The false ceiling in my hall is there to hide the warren of pipes that once serviced the whole block – hence the disproportional amount – and it has built-in lights covered by sliding panels of frosted glass. When I change the bulbs I can see the whole ugly mess, as this has to be accessible to both plumbers and builders. So imagine my horror when I came back from my daily walk to discover that the panel above my door had been removed and there was now a huge gap big enough for someone to crawl through and enter my flat via the false ceiling (he or she would only have to slide the glass panel and they would be in my hall). Admittedly two pipes were sticking out (one eight inches above my head) but it was nevertheless possible to access my flat without knocking on the door.

I was told that the pipes had to come out, as they were obsolete. So here we go again. I said that I wouldn't move out whilst this work was done so perhaps the answer was just to cap them off as they weren't doing anyone any harm and once I left (IF I left), then they would be taken out anyway. No one could argue with that so, eventually, capping them was what they did (a flimsy hardboard panel was erected for several weeks prior to the work). Again, this all took a long time and I had to suffer the fear of intruders for several months. I felt as though I was on one of those assault courses where just to get through it is the only objective, the downside being in my case that if I threw in the towel, it wouldn't just be a sense of failure I'd have, but I would also lose my home.

I'd survived floods, industrial drills, sledgehammers, asbestos, loose cables, water rationing, hoists, scaffolding, choking dust, broken windows, round the clock darkness, broken glass, lethal tools, intimidating solicitors' letters, threatening solicitors' letters, invasion of privacy, potential burglars, slippy floors and nooses and one large cockroach (although several smaller ones spring to mind also.) I really didn't see where things could go next so maybe finally I was going to get that fair offer, as I was ready to leave. Not quit, but move somewhere now more tenant friendly.

Several weeks went by without much more than a bit of light drilling and the occasional SMASH! SMASH! of a sledgehammer. Refreshingly peaceful, but would it last? It's the not knowing that does my head in and no doubt part of the psychological plan to wear me down.

At least once 'the letter' arrived I could get back to a sort of normality to – so *this* is what's happening next.

I had to let a man in who would ride around my flat on a sort of lawnmower, which would detect the spaces or voids that had possibly opened up under my concrete floor. Voids had been found elsewhere in the basement area so it was more than likely that I would also have them. This was obviously the trump card and for one teeny second I knew I was beaten. Of COURSE there were voids under my floors, fucking Carlsbad Cave sized voids, it was called the Circle Line. Battle weary I wrote back to arrange a time for the floorshow. I had learnt through experience that I couldn't deny the landlords entry if it were a health and safety issue, and ostensibly this was. I wasn't even going to argue the toss at this stage. I arranged for lawnmower man the next day. He came. He saw. He concurred.

The full horror of what was about to happen hit me with the force of next door's sledgehammer.

The landlords' letter two weeks later affirmed my worst fears. The remedial work would necessitate vacating my flat *with* all my furniture and furnishings for about ten days. I would be put up in an hotel, my possessions in storage. Leave my flat totally empty, in other words. Back to the assault course then, only this time it felt like I was scaling a mountain in flip-flops.

I knew that I was going to have to get a solicitor soon but, for a while at least, I could stall. One thing about my landlords that was in my favour was that they took an age to answer correspondence, partly I suspected because the points I raised usually meant conferring with solicitors (and we all know how longwinded that can be), as I did make valid points that they would have to be careful about checking.

My first letter pointed out that I hadn't in fact seen evidence that my floors needed attention and I wanted a copy of the lawnmower man's report on the laser machine's findings. Sure enough, the reply was not hurried. When it did come, it was not what I'd asked for; more a brief technical summary that said nothing specific. So again I wrote saying that I wanted to see an actual copy of the laser search report. Obviously no one wanted me to see it because I then received a copy of the landlords' consulting engineer's summary regarding the general state of the basement floor slab as a whole. It was the final paragraph of this summary that really confirmed my suspicions:

'The generally poor support found throughout the basement area suggests that, depending on the intended use of the floor, remedial measures should be considered to reinstate the support of the slab. Solutions involving stabilisations of the sub base while minimising the additional imposed loads may assist in avoiding further problems of deconsolidation and self compaction.'

A lot of 'ifs', 'buts' and 'maybes' there. The laser report would have to confirm that my area was voided to a level that was beyond dispute, otherwise there didn't appear to be any urgency at all. Had I not had several years of dealing with attempts to get me out of my flat, allegedly for remedial work, then the above report would have possibly blinded me with science and I would have complied immediately, fearing possible eviction if I didn't.

I wrote back yet again (I have tenacity if nothing else). I pointed out that the obviously laid-back summary meant that I wasn't going to drop into the abyss that appeared to be opening up beneath my feet just yet, so until I saw the laser report, I would not respond to any other correspondence.

I knew that it would take some time to perhaps 'mock up' a satisfactory account of the findings (I've had to look at all possible scenarios, it's not just cynicism), so I felt able to get on with my life in the interim. I even felt slightly euphoric in an odd sort of way. I'd thwarted what must have looked like a watertight plan to secure the flat finally and quickly. I wasn't a pushover and I wasn't stupid and if they hadn't realised that before, they did now.

Nevertheless, I suspected the battle wasn't over yet and I needed a break before the next phase. For months I 'd been plagued by mouth ulcers – a sure sign of stress – and frequent chest infections from the clouds of dust thrown up by the massive building works surrounding me, so I needed a change of air at least. Sevenoaks may not be the Italian Riviera, but for a couple of days it would be as good as. After that I was going to stay with a friend in Dorset for a few days hopefully – there was always the chance I would bore her rigid as she had her own problems to cope with and I might be put on the return train that same day.

I went to see Rebecca and Sean in Sevenoaks regularly. They were a great support and it was a joy to see Rebecca so happy. Although only twenty-two, Sean was already the manager of a well-known restaurant nearby. His parents were hoteliers so he had been around catering from an early age. I'm not mad about eating out as I know what can go on behind the scenes of even exclusive establishments as all my daughters have worked as waitresses at sometime or another in their lives (even Susie), but Sean's place was a germ-free, sterile palace. He was adamant that any food left over at the end of the day (and I'm talking unprepared) must be thrown out regardless. Knives were never used on more than one item of produce and cleanliness in the kitchen was of the highest order. I would have been happy to have an emergency operation in there any time, safe in the knowledge that the meat cleaver was spotless.

Sean is a good looking young man – he reminds me of the actor John Simm (no one ever sees my comparisons, Rebecca says that Lenny Henry looks more like Simm than Sean does) – he has a dry sense of humour and a pleasant approachable manner. He is unflappable but positive – qualities essential in running a busy restaurant. He also never took advantage of his position and always paid for family and friends to eat there so we didn't make a habit of it, but when we did, it was a real treat.

This particular night, despite my ulcers, I agreed to sample the new menu. There were two guys being offensive to the waiter for no reason as far as we could see. They had obviously been drinking but not so that they were out of control. Dean went up to them and politely asked what the problem was. One replied, "This fucking wanker's deaf, pal, we've been trying to attract his attention for ten minutes, you should get rid of him and if you don't, we just might."

Sean replied calmly, "Actually, you were clicking your fingers at him for *two* minutes, but he's not a dog so he wouldn't respond to that. I think therefore I would like to get rid of *you*." They refused to go so Sean called the police. They came in a matter of minutes and escorted the incensed, protesting pair outside. I only wished they'd got 'our gendarmes' as they'd be eating dust, never mind steak tartare.

Waiters and waitresses have a rotten job. The hours are long, the pay poor (tips are frequently meagre). The work is unrewarding as often they are treated like invisible servants who do not merit even a please or thank you. They are doing a job like anyone else for God's sake. And it can't be due to a feeling of superiority that tipping might engender, as hairdressers are *fawned* over *and* tipped massively on many occasions.

Doing obscene things to the food on the menu is essentially folklore, but could you really blame an abused waiter if he serves up Ham and Pee soup? Eating at my place isn't exactly without its hazards. I've already mentioned the cat debacle but even worse was the time I cooked a green pan scrub in a casserole. I don't know how it fell in there but it blended perfectly with the green peppers so I didn't spot it until it was time to dish up. I thought I would have to throw the whole lot out – but I only had some marmalade and an ancient tin of frogs legs in the cupboard and I didn't think they would make a good substitute, however tres nouvelle cuisine it might appear. So in a panic I rang a friend – cordon bleu trained – who said it would be all right to serve, minus the pan scrub unless anyone needed colonic irrigation.

I'm sure that everyone has disaster stories to tell. I do remember the night when a friend had forgotten to include herself in the head count of a dinner party she was giving. Rather than embarrass everyone, she simply toasted a thick piece of bread, added garnish, and bingo, she had a beef fillet just like the other guests. A disaster averted then, but coffee wasn't quite so successful as she made it with gravy granules. I knew it would happen one day because she hadn't got round to labelling her glass storage jars.

Marilyn lived in a picture book cottage near Dorchester and I was looking forward to catching up on some sleep, as it has to be the quietest place on earth. We were hopefully going to do nothing more than laze around in the pretty garden bordered by fields, with hills in the distance.

Dan and I had the stand next to Marilyn and her husband Matt at an antiques fair in Sussex and we became good friends. We spent the odd weekend with them and they were both hospitable and great company. We'd known them for about five years when Dan and I split up. I hadn't told anyone outside of family as I couldn't bring myself to even talk about it without bursting into tears so I carried on doing Portobello Road and the fairs on my own, fending off awkward questions the best I could – I usually said he was in the studio working on an album.

The fair came around (there are only four or so a year) and I set up as usual – well not quite as usual as I couldn't carry the normal amount of stock that we would have taken, as I had to get the tube to Waterloo and another train to

Esher, then either take a taxi or walk perhaps a mile to the showground. Marilyn arrived and we barely had time to acknowledge each other, thankfully, as the dealers were buzzing around looking for things they could in turn make a profit on. I still had decent stock in those days so I took three hundred pounds in the first hour and Marilyn appeared to be selling as well. Business was a lot brisker in those days. Marilyn's sister was helping instead of Matt, so I asked if he was ill but Marilyn said that it was Pinks, her boxer, who was sick and Matt was looking after him. It should have clicked then, as Marilyn would never have left her 'baby' when Matt could have done the fair. He was after all a great salesman, tall blond and very good looking. Women dealers couldn't resist his appealing patter. Men liked him too, and would enjoy swapping trade anecdotes. Marilyn was much quieter, always beautifully groomed (she used to be a fashion designer), shyly attractive, content to let Matt hold court. She is one of the most conscientious and loyal people I have ever met; a wonderful friend, and I am lucky to have met her.

I trotted out the studio excuse to Marilyn and was relieved that her sister Vicky was a useful buffer as she sat between us, rendering anything other than small talk an impossibility. Marilyn certainly seemed in a bit of a state though and when she went to the tea bar I said to Vicky, "I don't want to say anything to Marilyn because she is obviously very upset about Pinks and I don't want to upset her any further, but Dan and I have split up."

Vicky was shocked. "Marilyn and Matt have split up, too."

Well, how unbelievable. I had to say something even though I knew that we would both be very emotional (not the right place for a sisterly show of feelings). Predictably, we both burst into tears and Vicky had to man both stands whilst we composed ourselves in the car park.

Matt and Marilyn had been together since they met at Art College, so some twenty years. Their marriage was to all intents and purposes a successful one. So what had gone wrong? At a party just four weeks before, Matt had met up again with a girl he had gone out with for a short while back in the sixties, before Marilyn, and they both decided that the relationship wasn't over. And so he moved out the next day and went to live with her.

Eventually Matt would leave her – inevitable in the circumstances – and want to go back to Marilyn. I think at first Marilyn would have had him back, but it was far enough down the line for her to have grown strong again, so she said no. She met Bob, her current partner, some time later and he is so right for her. Wonderfully kind and supportive, he truly adores her.

I've been thinking about Heroes since speaking to Jonathan and wondering who I would choose if I were famous. It would be impossible to single out just one person and I'm amazed that the people taking part in the series didn't give me a long short-list, if you see what I mean. In no particular pecking order, the following are just some of my heroes:

Possibly because I'm not religious and maybe also because I was made to feel ultra special as a child, I've never felt the need to try to justify my existence or attach any deep meaning to it. As far as I'm concerned I'm here and when I'm gone, that's it, end of story. I would love to have my mother's blind faith that one day she will be reunited with my father in heaven. It gives her a serene passage through the here and now – and I could sure do with some of that at this moment in time. But nevertheless I am spiritual, albeit on a different level. I am not an empty vessel. I feel, perversely, sublime when I contemplate my insignificance in the awesome universe. How magnificent to be so overwhelmed. To be a mere speck is so utterly thrilling.

Scientist, Professor Richard Dawkins, most famous perhaps for his compelling book *The Selfish Gene*, also appears to be unconcerned about his place 'in the great scheme of things'; rather he "cares about what's true about the universe." It would be so inspiring to meet this eloquent, brilliant man.

Despite the hiatus in my own writing, my passions are stirred by music. It's my joy, my sadness. Music heals, music can for that moment in time be my raison d'etre. I have a catholic taste, from Gregorian Chants to Heavy Metal, mood dictating the choice. One of the many artistes who has touched my soul is K.D. Laing. She's a lesbian, I'm not. But she reaches the parts that not many have.

K.D. Laing

If I were a man

I could really fall for you.

I would love to meet Bill Bryson on the road to anywhere, carry his flask, save him from Grizzly bears and grizzly bores. This man has pulled me back from the edge on dark days – it's hard to feel suicidal for long when every sentence that he writes is a howler.

"If you're caught in a rip," Deirdre was saying, "the trick is not to panic."

I looked at her. "You're telling me to drown calmly?"

I would love to reproduce every word of every book he has ever written for those who have never discovered him but I'm not sure how the royalties would work. I do know that he sure beats Prozac; he's a habit I don't want to kick.

I dreamt last night that the workmen had started working outside of the flat again. I could see them clearly as a window had suddenly appeared in my sitting room wall. At that moment, the chap from the flat above appeared. He didn't say 'Hello, do you mind if I walk through your flat?' He just ignored me. Anyway, he couldn't find the door so he had to eventually speak. I asked what he thought he was doing and he said that he couldn't stand meeting the workmen so he wanted to exit through my flat.

Later on I went up to his floor to see what the problem was. The fire escape was his front door, so I went out and discovered a roof area which I noted would be good to use on days when I couldn't be bothered to go in the park, despite the fact that it looked like a rubbish tip. I went for a walk and I met a young girl who asked me to help inflate her hood. I was a bit suspicious of this and when two of her friends suddenly materialised I knew I was in trouble. The first girl was about to nut me when I grabbed her and smashed her head on the floor. This knocked her out and the others ran off.

I went back downstairs and found several workmen in my hall cooking their lunch on my oven. I went mad at this intrusion, but they were most indignant, saying they had to eat – which put me in my place. A revving motorbike outside woke me up.

I used to have great memory recall, remembering every dream in minute detail and I really enjoyed the action replay when I woke up – it was better than going to the cinema sometimes. These days I have difficulty remembering even fragments let alone the whole dream, the aforementioned is an exception to the rule and maybe it's a good thing as these are the sort of dreams/nightmares I have had for a few years now – the theme, invasion of my privacy. It doesn't need a psychoanalyst to work out why.

I'm still riding those infernal buses though.

At least I've been writing – mainly rubbish but then I have to justify not selling my piano. Here's one I think is promising:

IF PEOPLE ONLY KNEW

*Verse*
    You sit in your ivory tower
    Playing the part so well
    You know that you've got the power
    You've got me in your spell
    If people only knew what we do
    Imagine what they'd say
    You're so respectable
    Everyone knows your name
    Nobody sees the game you're playing
    If people only knew what we do
    Imagine what they'd say

*Chorus*
But when we close the blinds
Shut out prying eyes
Reservations go
You and I both know
Every night you've sat alone
The one you're with
Does not come home
You've turned to me
For sympathy and love
If people only knew what we do
Imagine what they'd say.

Don't ask.

# CHAPTER EIGHTEEN

The draining events of the last few years plus the incident with Keith, my mother's doctor, had really put me off sex. Not men obviously, as there are some fabulous men out there. (I know a lot of women who would disagree with me on that) but I only wanted to discuss the aesthetics of eighteenth century chandeliers with them, not swing from the bloody things.

I was going to have to snap out of this antipathetic state, otherwise I could easily become permanently repelled by the thought of sex. Already I had to look away from the television screen when people were kissing and if two people were actually in bed together, I had to change channels. Yuk, give me *Songs Of Praise* any day.

I'd met Jeremy a couple of years before, at one of the fairs. He wasn't a dealer but his mother was, so he came to the occasional fair to buy for her. He was about forty, attractive in a Brad Pitt sort of way – only joking, he looked more like Quasimodo. Joking again. He was plain. He did not stand out in the crowd fighting to get to the other stalls around me (these are now my junk days), but at least he didn't pass me by with that faint look of bewilderment and disgust that my goods now evoked. He picked up one or two things carefully (junk does not usually engender such respect). I liked him immediately. He settled for a turn of the century book on sunflowers. It transpired that he was a landscape gardener, divorced with two grown-up sons. He was forty-nine. I didn't fancy him at all when I first met him but I had started to find him attractive recently – although I still couldn't entertain the idea of sex.

I went out with him a few times and found him good company and interesting. We went to Kew Gardens and the

National Gallery together and as we both liked Van Morrison, we went to see him at Wembley. Inevitably sex reared its (still) ugly head and I made my excuses and left, as they say. The second time wasn't so easy but I still managed to come up with a plausible excuse.

When it did happen, it didn't. Jeremy simply couldn't rise to the occasion. Phew, what a relief. I told him convincingly that I didn't mind at all, first night nerves was a common thing. The second time it happened, I put it down to drink – and again I put him at his ease (although he was quite floppy already). Maybe it was the condom.

I was actually looking forward to our third attempt as the bit of practice had kick-started my libido again. I could tell straight away, however, that he wasn't going to make it. The condom hanging forlornly off his penis said it all. In the end, he took the only option left and suggested that oral sex might do the trick (he was desperate just to get back to his sunflowers, I could tell), so I said gently, "I don't do oral sex, I'm a vegetarian." He was obviously thrilled and seized on my excuse – forgetting that we'd just eaten roast chicken, not nut cutlets. Also, let's face it; it would have been like sucking on a caterpillar.

These things do happen and it is boring, but most women will put up with it occasionally. However, if it happened too often of course, it would be posted on the Internet:

Jeremy is flaccid again

Perhaps he really fancies men

So I was back to square one, well not quite as I was now feeling worse that I had before, as the inevitable feeling of hopelessness was now exacerbated by such a disastrous outcome. It once happened to me before, many years ago, when I got involved with a married man but we worked out that it was our guilt making him impotent. (I believe I said things like 'Don't you feel terrible that you're cheating on your wife?' and his response would be 'I shouldn't be doing this', instead of foreplay banter.) I don't know *what* Jeremy's excuse was.

The latest on the voids front arrived, so I didn't have time to dwell on things like coitus interruptus when my floors were facing cementus interruptus. The laser map did indeed appear to be a work of fiction. There are areas marked where the instrument never registered. The original brief was for the site to be sectioned into a grid pattern, but rather than move my grand piano, that area was left untested as indeed were similar sections in other rooms. I wrote back querying this discrepancy, wondering if perhaps I'd been sent someone else's map by mistake.

Meanwhile, I was in my corner shop when in came the management's Mr. Two Hats – oleaginous/arrogant. He gushed over to me and said, "Mrs. Walters, how are you?"

"It's Ms. Francis. And I'm not very happy."

He ignored this and continued, "I've been trying to ring you this morning but your 'phone was engaged."

"It happens."

"Have you had a chance to study the report yet?"

I was quite startled. Trapped by the photocopier, I wanted to scream for help. Instead, I said through gritted teeth, "Yes, and as I've already said – several times – it isn't conclusive, therefore I see no compelling reason to leave my flat."

"I know you think that we're trying to get you out, but I assure you we're not."

I was amazed that my business was being discussed near the Del Monte pineapple display in full earshot of customers and the shop's owner, Mr. Khan.

"I'm sorry, but I don't believe you. I think you are." And the more they pushed, the more I would dig my heels in, I told him, hoping that he would now go away and spare my blushes further. But to my amazement he continued, switching to the issue of the buy-out offer that I had turned down months before.

"I'll have a word with my clients, I'm sure they'll give you the extra five thousand." This was said in a very smiley-smiley, conspiratorial way. I thought he was going to hug me.

"Hang on, prices of property have gone up since that offer was made."

"I know my clients won't go higher. But we're happy for you to stay."

"Fine, I'll stay then."

I apologised to Mr. Khan for this untoward attempt at a business deal in his emporium, but the slippery customer next to me didn't so much as glance at him and his ham sandwiches in a 'there will be something in it for you, boy' sort of way.

"Look, let me have the letter you say you've written – for my clients – and then I'll have a word with them about the five thousand." The man just doesn't listen. He then slithered out of his new office back to his old one no doubt to report that he'd convinced me that they were not trying to get me out.

Mr. Khan said he had heard every word and yes, he was surprised at the impromptu meeting and he hoped I was alright.

You see, it's not just about getting enough money to buy a modest flat in a safe area (and I am entitled to that), but I have lived here for most of my adult life, brought up three children, and have a wealth of poignant memories. What's more, I've undoubtedly paid for the flat in full by now, so why should I do the landlords any favours? They bought the place with statutory tenants in it. I don't want to go (in normal circumstances, that is). I have been so very happy here, so one has to conclude that I *am* being forced out, as there's only so much that one can take before one's mental and physical health breaks down completely. I can't let that happen of course, but I don't feel I can concede yet. I have to fight for my rights. Justice is the spur.

But I do have a fucking awful headache. The 'meeting' must have done it. I wasn't going to accept the offer, so it was gloves-off time as just a few days later, I received a letter stating the urgency of the remedial work (not according to the landlords' own engineer's report some weeks previously). It looked like the whole block would fall down now if we didn't crack on.

I rang a friend who is a chartered surveyor and although he is not a structural engineer, nevertheless he has an overall knowledge. He knows my flat and has never noticed early warning signs of impending disaster, but he came round to double check – after all, he doesn't make a habit normally of looking behind curtains and lifting up edges of carpets. His verdict was that there wasn't any evidence to indicate that the extensive and disruptive remedial works proposed were essential at the time. He sent a report to me, which I then forwarded to the landlords, particularly underlining the following:

'Although it would seem from the report that the floor slab is unsupported in places, my inspection did not reveal any obvious visible defects resulting from this lack of support. Indeed one of the areas where tests have identified voids beneath the slab is the living room and in this room the floor is supporting the weight of a grand piano seemingly without adverse effects.'

Around the same time, a friend in Yorkshire had given me the name of a leading structural engineer, so I rang him on the off chance that he might give me some advice off the cuff.

He listened carefully to my account and asked to see a copy of the report. He said he would put his findings – allowing for the fact that his opinion would be formed without visiting the site – in writing. Aren't some people nice?

He more or less concurred with Stefan, my surveyor pal, just as I'd hoped. Still, might as well make it a hat trick. I rang a structural engineer in Scotland (Sean found him on the internet). His opinion was the same as Stefan's and Ian's but he also added that even if I had a party with a lot of people, the floor could compress slightly but would rise again (something like that), eventually. There was no problem should that happen.

The landlords did not acknowledge any of these findings. They must have had some effect though because suddenly everything went quiet again and it would be a couple of weeks before I heard from anyone (surely if walls are going to suddenly collapse I ought to be out of there, not being allowed to prevaricate).

I suppose it was inevitable that I should be so dismayed at my treatment as I was brought up with a strong sense of fair play, to rail against injustice and above all, to be truthful. I wasn't a goody two shoes, though – far from it. When I was about thirteen my friends (that 'wrong crowd' I got in with) and I used to go and nick things from Woolworth's after school. It was easy if you only took things on the edges, but the downside was that more often than not you'd end up with things like razor blades and shoelaces – stuff you didn't really want – so we'd put it all back the next day, on the wrong counters usually.

"Mummy, why are there razor blades in the sherbet dips?"

"I don't know, Elvis. Let's sue the bastards."

So sorry, Mr. Woolworth.

Actually, it was my father's fault because he always said that 'a liar is worse than a thief', so I didn't see much wrong with it at the time. Had he asked me if I'd stolen anything, I should have told the truth, of course.

When my mother heard (only recently) about my criminal past, she was shocked and disgusted – 'a daughter of mine' and all that, but I was amused at the pride with which she declared, "I wouldn't steal a pin."

Neither would I. A packet, maybe.

My father was brought up by his stepmother, as his own mother died giving birth to him. That affected him deeply all his life. He felt irrational guilt and because of this he was very protective towards my mother and was fearful that history would repeat itself when I was born.

He grew up in a part of Bradford called Idle. At the age of ten he passed a tough entrance exam and was awarded a scholarship (one of only two) to an exclusive boys' public school, Woodhouse Grove, but he refused to go because he said that he would be out of place. There was even more snobbery at these abodes in my father's day and as my grandfather was a bespoke tailor rather than a doctor or lawyer, he more than likely would not have fitted in, despite his sunny nature and good sense of fun.

He served an apprenticeship and became a master joiner but was eventually persuaded to join his uncle's soft drinks firm until he found his true vocation as a fireman. He rose swiftly up the ranks and even spent time in London in the Thames fireboats. I used to love it when he let me ride in the fire engine with him (you don't see much of that these days) and ring the bell.

He once bought me a three-wheeler bike (so I must have been about four) from a fellow-officer but took it back when he caught me riding in the road with my feet on the handlebars. The road to the station was very steep and very long, so he jumped on the bike and freewheeled down. Carr Lane was also very busy, so it must have caused some consternation as he was in full uniform. I can just see the headlines now, 'Cutbacks in Shipley Fire Service have resulted in Section Leader Bill Francis, father-in-waiting of Rag Queen, Lily Francis – having to replace fire engines with tricycles. Customers will have to provide their own water from now on.'

He met my mother when he was in his late twenties. She was nineteen and it was love at first sight – indeed, they were soul mates until the day he died. My mother was adopted and had always felt insecure until she met my father. Her adoptive parents had hinted but never told her about her background, so these kindly but misguided people had fomented her nagging doubts. They married after a short courtship and a year later I arrived to complete the happy picture.

Perhaps it was the fact that my mother had been adopted that made her so over-protective, suffocating even. She has since said that she should have had another child as it wasn't fair on me, but at the time she only wanted to love me unconditionally.

Sometimes when my father chastised me – and I always deserved the ticking off – my mother would say, "Leave my child alone."

My father would reply, "She's my child as well, love."

Despite being 'wrapped in cotton wool', I was allowed to do everything I wanted within reason. When I was sixteen I went twice a week to a club in Bradford and bopped my socks off until it finished at 10.30 p.m. I had to be in by eleven and I respected that so I was never late (I wouldn't have been allowed to go again if I was – I was never smacked, just deprived of treats). I had to pass a cricket field to get to my house and one night I saw the shadow of a man in a trilby hat behind me. I quickened my pace, so did he. I broke into a run and he grabbed me round the neck. I screamed in sheer terror and he let go, saying, "Lily, it's me, David." It was my friend's boyfriend. He'd been waiting for me, as he knew I came back at that same time. He said he'd done it for a joke. Sick bastard.

That was the last time I ever walked home alone late at night (I still don't) as my father always met me after that. I was allowed to take boyfriends home, but more often than not I didn't as they'd say, "Anyone you feel you can't bring home probably isn't right for you."

The trouble was I didn't always feel like going out with a non-swearing, non-drinking, church-going member of the Young Liberals.

I dyed half of my fringe peroxide blonde. The other half, like the rest of my hair, I left its natural reddish-brown colour. I also painted on thick black eyebrows, which, according to my parents, made me look like someone called George Robey, a latter day music hall artiste. I thought I looked fabulous (and so did the drinking, swearing, heathens I consorted with). My father was so ashamed of me that he once crossed the road when he saw me in the city centre rather than have to speak to me in public. My appearance combined with my affected scowl made him remark to my mother on another occasion, "I've just seen our Lily, she looked as though she'd just murdered someone."

He adored me really and was just as proud of me as my mother was, but unlike her, he didn't shout it from the rooftops. It was so embarrassing hearing my mother brag about everything I did when it was just normal kids' stuff. In vain I would remonstrate, "Sheila can catch a ball too Mummy, can you tell the newspaper about her as well?" (I'll get a slap when my mother reads this.)

My father died of a brain tumour aged just fifty-seven. My mother has never got over it to this day. She certainly didn't want to get married or even have a relationship again. "No one could ever take the place of your lovely father." Her inscription on his headstone says it all: 'He was Steadfast, Loyal, Faithful and True.'

My main regret is that he didn't know me when I was a bit older, wiser and hopefully, nicer. He had all that teenage crap instead. And I missed out on really knowing just how wonderful he was. My first real glimpse was at his funeral. The church was packed and his friends and former colleagues were openly weeping – and it takes a lot to make a man cry in public. As one of them said to me afterwards, "You see Lily, Bill was that rare kind of person who could communicate with anyone – tramps or kings – because he had humility and compassion. And he had a fearsome intellect, you know."

I didn't really. What teenage girl does? He's your Dad, who doesn't think drinking ten bottles of Tetley's Bitter is a good thing and so grounds you for a week. Where's the compassion in that?

Life's a bitch.

# CHAPTER NINETEEN

I've had a 'phone call from an old boyfriend who lives in Spain now but is in London for a few weeks so we are going to meet up. Roy, who is a dead ringer for Bob Mortimer (believe me, he is) is a rock photographer and during the seventies and eighties he was a regular face at clubs and music venues. I'd be there with my tape recorder and he'd be there with his camera so it was inevitable that we would meet – I think we once 'cornered' Paul Weller at the same moment. Some of the images are familiar all over the world as they appear on all kinds of merchandise from T-shirts to shower curtains.

The first time we really got together was at a record company promotional do. Back in the early eighties these events were usually lavish affairs with mountains of splendid food and champagne by the bucket load. On this particular night I vaguely remember wandering around with two bottles of Belle Epoque and meeting Roy who offered to run me home. I was obviously pretty paralytic as I'd reached the stage of bumping into things and hugging long-lost friends (people I'd been with five minutes before), so I was ready to go.

I felt very queasy but sixth sense said I mustn't throw up over Roy's car so I turned my head away and was sick very quietly down the left side of my coat. My 1940's (supposedly once Joan Crawford's gorgeous, duck-egg blue, moygashel) coat. I recall feeling very pleased with myself thinking Roy would never know. When we got to the entrance of my block, I was astounded that he wouldn't drive to the front door.

"But I can't, there are ten steps up" he probably said. I told him that it didn't matter and just to drive up them. The next thing I remember is sitting in the bath in just my tights and slip, picking 'diced carrot' from my hair and repeatedly muttering something like 'Yuk'. I think Roy then came in and washed my hair and that was it until the telephone woke me the next morning. It was Roy ringing to see how I was. What could I say? I thanked him for washing my hair and obviously not leaving me to sit in the bath all night. I was sure he would never want to see me again, but he did.

He said, "We've all done it, it's just one of those things."

Yes but no one is that magnanimous usually. I must have looked utterly revolting (and I didn't exactly smell of Chanel No.5) but obviously, like looks, vomit is merely skin deep to a thoroughly decent chap like Roy.

We went out together for a couple of years or so and they were some of my best times ever. When Dan and I got married, Roy took the official photos as a wedding present – more reason for feeling sad when I look at them, it was such a wonderful day. Roy even stayed the night along with my mother, Dan's brother, sister-in-law and nephew. A crowded start to the honeymoon.

I was right about the landlords taking a couple of weeks to come up with another 'frightener' and this one seemed to be the coup de grace.

I had queried why the work – should I be forced to agree to it by law eventually – couldn't be carried out room by room, my furniture simply moved around. The reply from Mr. Two Hats was along the lines of poisonous gases would be released when the injection process was under way and also that the technicians needed unobstructed access. It appeared that the men would have to wear protective clothing and should they inadvertently breathe in the hazardous fumes, hospitals would be on standby. All very scary stuff. It really was time for a solicitor so, with renewed enthusiasm, I set about finding one. Meanwhile, I still didn't believe that the work was essential, as contradictory reports still arrived.

One implied that the voids only affected the slab so there was no implication for the foundations, therefore the rest of the building would be perfectly sound. However, if the voids were left untreated below my flat, the effect was likely to be cracking and settlement of the floor slab, with my internal partitions also becoming unstable, which could result in sudden collapse. And I suppose if this happened, I could be watching *Newsnight* one minute and on it the next – 'Wall buries one of our viewers'

I didn't like to ring any of the people who had generously advised me before, particularly as there had been no feedback, so I looked in Yellow Pages for structural engineers. The first two I spoke to both dismissed the idea of toxic fumes and ambulances but couldn't make a proper overall judgement without seeing the site. Their fees, although definitely worth every penny, were beyond me. I rang another company and the chap I spoke to said, "Do you have cracks in your walls?"

"No."

"Then the work doesn't sound necessary to me. I'll come over and take a look."

I told him that I didn't think I would be able to afford him but I was grateful for his opinion as it strengthened my determination to carry on fighting. He replied in a tone that implied he was amazed that I should think such a thing.

"I don't want paying. I hate injustice and this sounds like a typical landlord ploy to me. I'll come over now."

He was as good as his word. He came in like a man on a mission. He beamed at me in a shortsighted way, barked, "Harry!" and strode into my hall.

"Beautiful walls," he murmured, stroking them tenderly. "Do you have beautiful walls in your other rooms?" We wandered around, marvelling at them together, at their symmetry, the uncanny way they held up the ceiling without a hint of buckling under the strain, how they were attached so firmly to the floors that not even a dust mite could have squeezed in.

"A woman on her own, vulnerable – I've seen it many times."

"So what am I going to do?" I implored.

"Nothing." He beamed wider. "Let them take you to court. I'll represent you."

I couldn't believe my amazing luck, to have found an ally – a 'gung ho' one at that. He said to send him all the current and future correspondence and he would handle things from now on. I explained again that I couldn't pay him and I wasn't comfortable about accepting his help unless I could. He was oblivious to my protestations and, still beaming, left on an even greater high than when he came. It looked like he was going to get involved whether I wanted him to or not – and to be honest, it was such a relief to feel that I had such a staunch supporter. I never thought to question his motives further as he was so obviously thrilled at the prospect of pitting his wits against the bullies.

Two days later I received a copy of a fax that he'd sent to the landlords' solicitors simply stating that 'This work is unnecessary.' When the solicitors' next letter threatened legal action if I didn't comply in ten days, Harry was beside himself with glee. I wasn't quite so happy and said I really must get a solicitor on the case as well. He was very insistent that I left it all to him as, more often than not, solicitors weren't to be trusted and he knew as much as they did anyway. I tentatively queried his qualifications but he merely reiterated that he could deal with it. He had a very persuasive manner and I found him very likeable but he was definitely eccentric, a real one-off. He was fiftyish, well educated, attractive and looked like the actor Paul Nicholas. He was divorced, lived alone, but had a regular girlfriend. She clearly adored him even though he was like an unruly child revelling in the attention. I had realised by now that he was a control freak – he had admitted this but said I had done everything he wanted me to do anyway. To demonstrate just how much in control he was, he left a shirt for me to wash one night (he said his machine had broken down). I said I wouldn't do it, but he said I would. And of course I did. After all, he was doing my work for free so how could I refuse? I'd only known the man for a few weeks and I was already doing his washing.

He certainly caused the landlords to back pedal though, because they suggested a meeting between both sides' engineers. Harry insisted that there was no need as there was nothing to discuss, he had stated his professional opinion and saw no reason to reiterate it face to face. However I said that I thought he should, otherwise it would look as though the other side were trying to be accommodating and we weren't. He reluctantly agreed but said that it would cost them £500 for his time. I totally freaked at this but he said that they had called the meeting and that was his fee. After a lot of debate they finally agreed to pay him. And guess what – he then gave the money to me. "You need it more than I do," was his justification. Such a strange, unarguably generous man, but I never knew what he was going to do next. He stalled the meeting over and over again – partly because he was indignant that his assessment was being questioned and partly because other things came up. I couldn't force him as I was totally beholden, but I was terribly concerned that a court summons would arrive (even though Harry wanted to go to court, I most certainly didn't). The strange thing was that the landlords bluffed and threatened but allowed Harry to mess them about for two or three months. Again I saw that there really was no urgency or writs would have been flying. However, I did think that as we now had the money it was only fair that we honour our part of the bargain. Being an honourable chap, he finally agreed and a date was set.

In the interim I learnt that Harry was a manic-depressive and regularly saw a leading Harley Street specialist. Now why wasn't I surprised? He was constantly having to change his medication and I could calculate by his behaviour when he needed to do this. Sometimes he just didn't bother to take it and this would have the same effect. His opinions would become grander and unequivocal, brooking no rational discussion. Once the balance was sorted he was delightful company and an inspiration. The trouble was my own mental health was under pressure and having such a loose cannon around was a really bad idea. I now longed to resolve the voids issue and there were moments when I no longer cared which way it went.

I have to say that Harry was brilliant at the meeting. He pulled out all the stops, arguing points that there really were no answers to, only weak supposition. Unfortunately at the end of the day it was a case of our word against theirs. And as the landlords' engineers had all the pre-requisite qualifications – not to mention a history with the block over years – that was all the landlords would need to convince any judge that I was obstructing essential remedial work. The one excellent thing that did come out of it was that the chap Harry had the meeting with happened to be the managing director of the company and had not been dealing with the fine details, so he said there was no problem with moving from room to room, the job would just take longer.

It really was obvious now that the landlords were using this as a ploy as the delays were in part to do with my insistence that I didn't want to leave the premises with all my furniture. If the work was so urgent and it was possible to do it this way (it would take two weeks rather than ten days – so what?) then if there *was* no hidden agenda they would have agreed to my demands. I had received legal advice in the past stressing the importance of not vacating my flat as landlords could find ways of preventing re-admittance. They could say that there were ongoing problems with the foundations and I wouldn't be able to prove it as even Harry couldn't get involved for free on that level. I wasn't married to the man; I only washed the occasional shirt, for Christ's sake.

It was probably true that there were voids that should be dealt with at some time or other (the opposing engineers were reputable, apparently) but there was obviously no urgency, my walls were not about to fall down. No wonder I was so terribly suspicious. Hidden agenda was writ large in flashing neon.

It really was time to get that solicitor. Harry would not be pleased but I had to have proper legal advice now if the work was to go ahead. I still didn't feel in the clear despite the prospect of remaining in situ. I would have to have Harry or someone to stand over the technicians to check that nothing dodgy was going on.

I should have been a detective

Harry rang at 12.30 am. I was in bed, so not too happy when he said that he'd like to pop in. "Why are you ringing so late?"

"I want to see you," he purred.

"Where are you?" I asked cautiously.

"Outside of your window.

"What?" Ooh, creepy. "Go away. What are you doing there?"

"I'm on my bike. I've come over specially."

All the way from Streatham – I was horrified. "Well, you can go back. NO WAY are you coming in." I took the phone off and realised even more how much I wanted to stay in a block where structural engineers didn't get past the Armani suited porters (Harry had been quick to spot that the head porter always wore designer labels) unless they had their own front gate pass. Believe me, he'd tried to get one, but sixth sense told me not to hand one over despite his accusations that he was kept waiting like a common street trader each time. Already two of the porters had complained to me about his rudeness. I knew that he was now taking the whole situation personally, but he hadn't to take it out on the porters. He duly apologised to them; nevertheless I was very nervous now as I knew that he could go off at any moment.

We had an appointment with a solicitor someone had recommended. I knew it was risky taking Harry along, but I needed him to corroborate my story. He worked on a 'no win no fee' basis – Harry would later accuse him of working for the other side. The first thing Harry said was, "I'm not happy about going to see this man, he'll be a crook, like all of them."

Exasperated, I pulled my hand away (he'd recently taken to holding it like a fretful child would, or at other times like a possessive lover.) "Harry, stop this. You are not going to court as my structural engineer *and* my solicitor. The judge won't buy it."

"They're all crooks as well."

I really lost it and screamed back at him, "Are you going to behave, or not?"

"Yes darling," he replied meekly.

He didn't, of course. He spoke in a soft mumble so that Mr. Carson had to repeatedly ask him to speak up. And he wouldn't look at him, staring instead at the ceiling and walls so intently, like he was on a busman's holiday. Despite this, Fraser Carson agreed to take on the case with the proviso that I didn't bring Harry into his office again. He suggested at a later date that it would be better if Harry kept a low profile generally.

Harry was backing off anyway as he was going through one of his low periods, which always followed his highs, apparently. I wasn't sure whether I preferred the manipulative manic charmer or the withdrawn melancholic. Obviously he was in a dark place, but then so was I. And according to the landlords, if I didn't let the builders in, I'd be in an even darker place – through my floor.

Fraser studied everything carefully, concluding that I was definitely being harassed.

"However, it could take months or even years to prove it"

He then told me about a client he had in a similar situation. She won in the end but it had taken four years. Four years of her life; a long time but I was already two ahead of that, so it was a gloomy prospect. Anyway, he fired off a stern no-nonsense letter to the landlords' solicitors which made me feel a lot better. He also said that I should have someone to supervise the works.

Harry agreed to play devil's advocate – now why did I say that, I wonder? Freudian slip, but very fitting. I wouldn't want him to obstruct the work or rub anyone up the wrong way, so I began to have doubts about his suitability. I didn't want to upset him as he had been fantastically supportive, so I had a few sleepless nights trying to sort out the dilemma. It would resolve itself as Harry had to go away at the crucial hour (maybe he too had been looking for an out, as he was very pissed off that a solicitor was now in control of things.)

There were numerous issues to sort out on both sides so it would be another eight months before things were finalised (just how urgent can this remedial work be?) so like the sword of Damocles it hung over me casting long shadows

# CHAPTER TWENTY

I was in limbo again waiting for the solicitors to reach a satisfactory agreement. It seemed like I'd been treading water for years, my life on hold. I was really worried that I had lost my creative drive permanently as now my attempts at songs were becoming more 'Country' in tone – you know the sort of thing:

> Mary Lou went to town
> To buy herself a hoe-down gown
> It can't have been to impress me
> Cos my legs don't go below the knee
> I lost them in a little old war
> So I can't dance and holler no more (Yee Haw!)
> No I can't dance and holler no more (Yee Haw!)

I don't think I'll be setting that to music.

These lyrics, however, are sung to a variation of Land Of Hope And Glory (Country with a difference):

There's a man at my door
> Wanting to dig up my floor
> Wearing a surgical mask
> All dressed up for the task

> No one seems to know
> What's in store below
> He could be in for a shock
> When he pops up at Ayers Rock.

God, I bore myself.

Fortunately Kelly came to the rescue (he might not, had he known how low my creative thrust had sunk). It wasn't much but at least it was professional and rather interesting. Kelly was now producing programmes for Classic FM, mainly recording concerts, so there wasn't any regular work going, but he did ask me to write some introductory programme notes. (I'm not quite as up on Schoenberg as I am on Radiohead – more familiar with Brahms and Liszt, the cockney version).

Kelly was originally a DJ. His weekend breakfast shows had a huge audience, as he was completely off the wall. He rarely planned anything and sometimes would play the B-side of a Top Twenty record by mistake and not even notice until bemused listeners rang in. He was more interested in folk music at the time and justified playing an unusually high proportion of this minority listening on the most popular show of the day by saying, "Mrs Jones in Tottenham, doing her ironing, wants to hear Davey Arthey and The Furies, not Motorhead."

But what about Bob junior in Ealing, eating his cornflakes?

"He doesn't get up until noon at the weekend, so that's Mike's problem." Mike was the next programme's DJ. Kelly was a hard act to follow.

Portobello is so bad at the moment that I haven't covered my rent for three weeks now. It's one thing to break even, but when the place is costing me money that I don't have, then it's serious. The trouble is, I can't afford to give up as, ridiculous as that sounds, I need the cash flow, albeit modest. I have managed to get my outgoings down to just under forty pounds per week (excluding rent and council tax) so I have to bring at least that much home every Saturday – and I do, but then my capital is being eaten into and I am finding it difficult to put it back, so my stock is therefore decreasing. I cannot buy things any cheaper – and still be commercial – than I am doing. Where does one go after charity shops and car boot sales? I know that the pattern will change and I won't keep on losing money but nevertheless it's very worrying when it happens. At least I can have a good laugh there and I always do the *Telegraph* crossword, which keeps my brain functioning, as it's quite a difficult one on a Saturday (well it is to me).

My arcade has seen some changes over the years but, on the whole, people do tend to stay as it is the first in the main body of the market, thus unavoidable, and it is also one of the first to open, so other dealers can come and hopefully buy before they set up later. Saturday would not be the same without a visit from the regular dealers known for their good humour. This week, for example, one wag said, "I sold a string of glass beads this week for twenty quid, only they turned out to be emeralds worth two grand, I heard later. As a result my wife's banished me to the spare room. So something good has come out of it."

Whenever business is bad, stallholders come up with various excuses, like, 'It's Harrods sale', 'It's the changing of the guard', 'It's too nice, everyone's in the park' (a dealer doesn't know what a park is, far too busy), 'It's the Grand National', 'It's the Notting Hill Carnival', 'Who wants to come to Portobello with all the bombs?' I usually say it's the government's fault as no one can afford my useless junk any more – that always gets a laugh.

Both dealers and members of the public bring 'antiques' around Portobello, hoping that someone will buy them. Often they are too expensive and not what we want anyway. However, there is another group of would-be vendors who have nothing whatsoever to do with antiques, but do at least brighten up an often tedious morning. There's a chap who sells anything from novelty hats to unusual safes. Last week he caught my eye (fatal) and asked if I was 'alright for talking parrots.' Then there's the androgynous character who offers 'caviar, 'Russian hats...' and Lord Somebody or Other with his cheap wine (eau de toilet). My personal favourite is an old Polish woman who always touts the unexpected, "Would you like to buy a little axe? Or a knitting bag?"

Then there are those who are not quite so amusing, the 'messers' – people who frequently ask to see something on the top shelf which means one has to balance precariously to reach the undesirable item (that's why it's been relegated to the top shelf). After a cursory examination, it's handed back with the immortal words, "I'm a collector and what I was really looking for was a moustache cup." The only crumb of satisfaction, if it's a woman, is to nod sympathetically and say, "It can't be easy using standard cups."

I always tell people that an item is cracked (and most of mine are) before I show it to them as it saves time and effort should they want it to be perfect. There are those, however, who insist on seeing the piece regardless then shake their heads, sadly saying they would have bought it if it hadn't had a crack in it.

Many dealers have 'day jobs' and manage to juggle the two satisfactorily. A love of antiques combined with a need to supplement perhaps a relatively low income makes it an attractive business to invest in. Actors and actresses can be out of work for weeks at a time and the extra income keeps them going. I knew a fire-eater who could afford to put real food on his table thanks to his Saturday job. Gavin, my next-door neighbour, is a set designer and rarely has to work on Saturdays so he's there most weeks. He's very funny and generous, always giving me bits to sell for him at ridiculously low prices so that I can make something on them as well. However, I won't be taking any of his stock to fairs again.

I took some of Gavin's things to a fair recently. I had the worst fair ever and only took sixty-eight pounds and I didn't sell a single brooch of Gavin's. As we were leaving, Emma happened to glance down at the floor under the table again (we always do check) and she noticed a bag that at first looked like a rubbish bag. It was Gavin's. It had slipped out of my stock bag at the latest minute. If she hadn't looked – and there was no reason for her to, as she'd packed her things well before I had – I would have owed him two and a half thousand pounds. The way things are going it would have taken me years to pay him back.

Portobello Road is a fascinating place, a bustling, colourful, giant Aladdin's Cave full of amusing characters. I wrote a synopsis for a reality style series based on Portobello and I took it to Greg Dyke when he was at TV-AM. He was very enthusiastic and thought it would work. He even discussed filming in our arcade every Saturday, fly on the wall stuff. Again, nothing came of it because he left shortly afterwards and went on to bigger and better things.

My mother's coming to stay this weekend and I've literally not got a penny to buy 'her' food (butter, lamb chops, Ambrosia creamed rice) – unbelievable I know. How much can that modest lot come to? Four pounds? She would make do with toast, but that's hardly a welcoming meal. I'll have to sell something else to Kieran, even though we're not really speaking at the moment.

He was pleased to hear from me but I was reminded six times of how horrible I'd been before he'd talk normally to me. Then he was very solicitous, "Of course I'll buy something to help you."

"Don't say it like that, as if you're doing me a favour – you benefit too – big time, no doubt."

"I've still got the pinball table."

"That's because you're hoping to get a better price from someone else you've got lined up."

"You're very cynical."

"I didn't use to be. It's the company I keep."

"Look, I'll *give* you some money, how much do you want?"

"That's very nice of you but I would be worried about the strings."

"Lily, Lily, Lily. Look, I wouldn't want much, just a small room at the back of your flat – not the front, so no strings."

He said that he would like to see Dorothy and he would bring her dinner in with him. I wasn't having that; for a start she didn't eat kebabs (and I knew it would be half-eaten) and she wouldn't want visitors on her first night. He said that he would bring her anything she wanted and he would go and sit in 'his' room when she arrived.

What an exhausting man. I said to send me twenty pounds on account and he could come over on Sunday. He asked why he couldn't come over straight away.

"Because I've just picked off all my eyelashes."

"Well, you've got limbs and a nose haven't you? Those will do."

I went to meet my mother from the train at King's Cross although I didn't usually. No, I let her struggle with her heavy bags on her own – nice daughter, I'll be sorry one day. Actually, I never usually know what time she's arriving as she likes to do the journey 'leisurely' (and she would try to carry my bag as well if I met her). Alan Bennett was coming through the barriers (he has a place in North Yorkshire) and as I knew my mother would be taking it leisurely down the platform, I went up to him as I'd heard somewhere that he collected clocks. He looked apprehensive when I approached him, he must have thought I was a stalker. Then I realised that I was wearing a fake leopard skin coat and I *was* at King's Cross – a pick up place in more than one sense – so he was no doubt expecting me to say, "Do you like a good time?" instead of "Do you like a good time-keeper?" Anyway, my information was wrong, he didn't collect clocks, good time-keepers, or otherwise. My mother was distraught that I'd 'let him go' before she'd had a chance to meet him.

"Oh heck, Lily, I'm very disappointed – you know I think he's great. I hope you told him you came from Yorkshire."

"You shouldn't have gone to all this trouble, love. A piece of toast would have done."

"No trouble, Mother," I bluffed.

"I don't know how you manage. I'll give you something before I go. And living in this dingy place, it's awful for you. I used to think it was lovely here, but it's so depressing now."

She was close to tears but then asked angrily, "And when are those damned things (scaffolding) going to be taken down? It's worse than being in Armley Jail."

"I didn't know you'd been inside, Mother – it must have just been for a long weekend. What did you do – knock a judge's wig off?"

"You daft thing. You're just like your father, same sense of humour." She was laughing now. "But you know one of the judges did lose his wig when I was there. He was scrabbling around for ages under the bench looking for it. Ooh, we did have some fun."

Apparently none of the policemen could say 'breath test' correctly, so it always came out in court as, "I said to the suspect, 'Mr. Smith I want you to take a breast test'." I wonder if that's nationwide or just in Bradford?

"Do you remember that time when you had to pass around a dildo – that must have been embarrassing in front of your magistrate friends and Ken the dog handler." (I was reminded of this because we were watching a programme with some of those fanciful contraptions being passed around a group of women who looked as though they'd be more at home sitting on a stair lift than one of those).

"I had to pass it to one of our coppers who was dying to laugh and I mouthed, 'It's dead but it won't lie down.' You should have seen his face." She laughed heartily at the memory.

A slob of a man was now talking about oral sex in great detail much to my mother's disgust, "It's absolutely revolting!"

"I agree, but you've heard it all in court."

My mother was very indignant, "That's different. It's police officers describing it, not horrible people like that."

Kieran came over the next day as arranged. My mother was pleased to see him as she thought he was good fun and would help me.

"Only if he moves into your bedroom" I told her. "Don't worry, it's not you he's after, he just wants that room."

Kieran was carrying a large bag when he arrived.

"For me?" I asked.

"Yes, it's some spare tools and a car battery."

"So not for me then."

"Yes, for your room, my room." He stood close up to my mother for support. "Lily's always wanted a ratchet, hasn't she Dorothy?" Then he remembered something he wanted to ask her. "Now Dorothy, is Alzheimer's contagious?"

She laughed and replied, "Don't ask me, I haven't got it yet."

Kieran thought for a moment then concluded, "I suppose it is if you catch it from your grandmother." He then opened his Coke fridge (like a child, he assumed I wouldn't tell him off in front of someone). "It's empty," he said incredulously. "What have you done with that twenty pounds? How many lamb chops did you have Dorothy, ten? Haven't you even got a cigarette for me?"

"You don't smoke."

"But I like to have one here."

"We don't want your smoke, my mother particularly will go mad."

She had gone to make Kieran a cup of tea so I told him about the time after her mother died when her father came to stay for a while (in between the acrobats and the Ghurkha). He had his own cosy bed sitting room with a real fire in winter. He smoked a pipe, which he would leave on his bedside table. However, my mother was worried that he might light up and fall asleep, so she would move it onto the mantelpiece. One day he had a slight stroke and fell into the fire reaching for the pipe. He wasn't seriously burned as my mother came into the room a second or two later – and he recovered from the stroke – but she felt terribly guilty about this and blamed herself. Afterwards, she developed a phobia about smoking and from that day she couldn't bear the smell. She went to see a Harley Street specialist about it but he was apparently looking at his watch every few minutes so she felt he was only interested in her money and not her problem. My father refused to give up his ten Woodbines a day as he thought it would be counter productive to the phobia, but for the rest of his life (another twenty years), he did either smoke outside or hold the cigarette so that the smoke would go up the chimney.

Kieran had brought my mother a book that he'd picked up in a house he was doing up, because it had a picture of Patrick and Carmen on the cover. It was about mixed race relationships. She was thrilled of course as it meant another trip to the *Telegraph & Argus.*

"It's dated 1992, well past its sell by date, you can't," I said."

"That doesn't matter. It's a lovely picture of Carmen. I've seen better of Patrick though."

"Did I ever show you the book cover I did, Kieran? You tell the story, Mother."

"Oh, this is funny. Rebecca was only about ten, I'd taken her for a few days to Majorca and we were in one of those gift shop places when she pointed to a bookstand and said, 'Look Nana, there's a picture of Mummy.'

I said, 'Eh? Where?' She took it off the stand and I said, 'That's not your mummy, she's not common like that.'

Adrian patted me affectionately and said, "She is."

My mother laughed and carried on, "Well, Rebecca insisted that it was, so I had to buy the book. It really wasn't our Lily. Anyway, we brought it back and you took one look – do you remember?" she said, addressing me now "And you said 'That's not me'. Go on, you tell the rest of it."

"But then the belt caught my eye and I started to remember it, a copper affair with a leather thong tie. So I studied the picture closer and realised that it was me. It was from a set of photographs that I'd had taken when I was in my teens, when I had short blonde hair and a Brigitte Bardot style pout. The book itself was a cheap thriller and I obviously looked the part so someone stuck my photo on the front in the hope that it would sell the book. And it did, you bought one, Mother. I still can't get over Rebecca knowing it was me when I didn't recognise myself even. I've still got it somewhere."

"It didn't do you justice," said my mother. "You've got a lovely face when you're not looking so awful."

"Sorry? What's that supposed to mean, Mother?"

"All this worry you've got, it's making you ill." She turned to Kieran and pleaded, "Can't you help her, she's in a right mess."

"I will," promised Kieran. "I've said that I'll move in so that I can look after her."

"He only wants my address, Mother. It looks better on his business cards than 'Shed, Field in Barnet.' I'm going to bed. Goodnight."

# CHAPTER TWENTY-ONE

My mother had got me worried now. I certainly didn't feel well but I hadn't for ages, so I'd sort of got used to it, but maybe I should go and see the doctor. I felt like such a hypochondriac as there were so *many* things wrong with me. Why couldn't I just have something proper like Chickenpox instead of stress related things? The symptoms were real enough but the cure wasn't as simple. Large clumps of my hair were falling out now (I'd so much that I didn't miss it, but if it went on for too long, I might), so at least that was something new to discuss. The doctor was concerned and reiterated that I *should* see another counsellor. I thought I'd better, otherwise he might have struck me off his patient list.

I had to go to a health centre in London's Soho Square. Clare was the counsellor I would be seeing for the next few weeks. She was in her late twenties, stunning looking and dressed like a catwalk queen. How very odd. She looked ready to party, not listen to my woes. I couldn't do it. I tried to make it sound like fun to match the ambience, but it's quite hard to talk about panic attacks in merry tones.

She actually said lots of intelligent textbook things, but there mustn't have been a chapter on ageing rock stars' ageing ex-wives who are now penniless and about to go under – under the floor that is, so I wasn't too cut up when she had to go back to her native Australia. In fact to be honest, I didn't give a XXXX.

I'd been invited to a twenty-fifth wedding anniversary party and decided to definitely go. I had become very anti-social again, cancelling things at the last minute – partly out of a 'can't be bothered' attitude and partly because I felt I'd bore the pants off everyone. However, Sue and Mike were two of my oldest friends and I wanted to be there to celebrate this milestone (they still looked like teenagers to me). They asked me to bring Dominic as they liked him a lot but after the silent night at the Mason's, I didn't want to risk it. Also we really had now drifted apart. As I said, Dominic had 'got religion' and sombrely discussing the Bible over a glass of milk wasn't my thing (I'd spent all my childhood and teenage years in chapel, so I'd done my bit for Christianity, I reckoned). There were still traces of the old Dominic, I discovered, when I asked if his new flat had a garden. He replied, "Unfortunately I have to bungee jump from the third floor into a window box." Shame really, still what the hell, we have to move on.

I went on my own as I knew there would be lots of people there that I would know. I normally can't bear going to things solo. I would rather never go out again than feel I have to tag on to a group who are clearly bonding really well without a stranger hovering on the edges uninvited. No one wants to give you a quick resumé of what's been said, so you stand there, either grinning inanely or nodding sagely, wishing – for once – that the floor WOULD open and swallow you up.

I hadn't seen John Leyton for years. He went into the restaurant business when his musical and acting career went into decline, and was very successful. He still does package tours with the Marty Wildes and Joe Browns, but the sixties revisited can only ever be a pastiche. Girls in their millions bought his records. He still looks good. "Hi, Johnny remember me?" He did (so I can't look that bad, Mother).

Songwriter Russ Ballard was also there and I really was thrilled to meet him as he wrote one of my all-time favourite songs, *So You Win Again*, sung by Errol Brown, lead singer with Hot Chocolate. It was a number one hit in 1977 and I have played it ever since as it reminds me of someone who still has a bit of my soul, bittersweet memories I can't shake off. When I first interviewed Errol I said how much I liked his songs – he wrote most of them – and how 'So You Win

Again' was my favourite. He said he didn't write that one. Lesson number one – always do your research unless you want to come across as an amateur prat.

I don't read horror stories, or rather I didn't until I met James Herbert, our top writer in this genre. Mike had known him for many years and even though I was aware of the friendship, I had never actually met him before now. He was eager to discuss music as he has quite a record collection picked up over years of browsing around old record stores.

"One of my greatest sources of pleasure is listening to fifties rock 'n' roll music – that dates me, doesn't it – I love Buddy Holly, it's amazing how fresh his stuff sounds today."

We talked together for a couple of hours. He's a fascinating man and I was enthralled by his anecdotes and breadth of knowledge. He's witty, talented and has great charm – he sure charmed me – and he's replaced (for the moment) James Woods as top favourite. He's not my usual type physically, but he has that indefinable *je ne sais quois* quality that wins every time. But it will be also unrequited, as he's been happily married to Eileen for over thirty years, not to mention father to three gorgeous girls. Still it was great while it lasted. And I can't wait to add *his* horror stories to my list of ongoing horror stories.

Two weeks prior to the date set for the remedial work to be carried out, I had a visit from the contractor who wanted to make some last minute checks. He turned up with Mr. Two Hats who was definitely in hand-wringing mode as he stood there smiling broadly. I soon wiped it off as I blocked his way.

"I don't want you in my flat," I told him. He blustered and looked suitably embarrassed, bluffing that my solicitor had said it would be OK. I didn't believe him but I let him in as I didn't want to have to ring up my chap and find that he had agreed this as *I* would have looked foolish then. The contractor (interesting word that – I wouldn't want anything with 'con' in my job description) suggested that the rooms should be done in sequence, two at a time or as long as it took per day. The men apparently were going to drill holes at regular intervals, insert tubes through which the special fluid would flow, filling up the voids in each section. As we were discussing the best ways of stacking the furniture, Mr. Two Hats made one last feeble attempt at winning me over, "I know you won't agree to this, but it really would be better for you if *we* stored your furniture and put you up in a nice hotel." I can see why he's the landlords' robot.

Judgement Day arrived. I had fought off this moment for so long and now it was knocking on my door – oh, that was my chap Marvin. At least he was early. I don't think I could have handled the men on my own. Marvin seemed very laid back, unlike myself pacing back and forth – it might be my last chance. A bloke called Chas had cleared the two bedrooms earlier so my hall was piled high. I could live with that – I would be sleeping three inches off the ceiling but at least I would be in my own home instead of the Landmark Hotel for ten days and *then* a fleapit probably for the rest of my life.

A large van drew up outside of my kitchen window. I read the name on the side and my heart sank. This was really it. No stay of execution after all. Two chaps were ushered in by the porters and Marvin introduced himself and explained that he would be popping in from time to time. Huh? A new one on me. I thought he would be teetering on the edges of the yawning chasms for the whole duration, not paying fleeting visits just now and again. The feeling of impending doom intensified. Marvin assured me that if any problem arose he would come over immediately, but he thought the men seemed fine.

They did, actually. And there wasn't a surgical mask in sight. They laughed at that thought and said their idea of protective clothing was a fig leaf. They knocked on and to my great relief didn't find anything 'suspicious' in either room and so, first day over, I was able to relax a little and even sleep a bit on my elevated bed.

Chas came before the men and, single-handed, moved the furniture back into the bedrooms. He moved the next phase swiftly and made certain that I had access to essentials like the oven and television, otherwise it would be a bleak evening ahead of me.

One of the technicians came from Shipley, where I was born. I couldn't believe my luck and knew then that everything would be all right. We reminisced about Shipley Glen and the little fairground there. I told him about the time when I took the girls there only to discover that it was closed for refurbishment. We spoke to the owner who was updating the slot machines, to ask what he was going to do with the old ones.

"Nothing," he said. "Throw them out." So we offered to buy them (twenty in all) but he said we could just take them. In the end he reluctantly took twenty pounds. They were mainly 'All-Wins' from the thirties and forties but one or two were novelty pin-up ones. I said that we should keep those and a couple of the others and give the rest as presents. Later we would discover that they were worth twenty-five pounds each (so I'm afraid friends had to make do with something more conventional in their Christmas stockings) and we sold them all in a local Saturday antiques market. From then on I caught the buying and selling bug and that's how I started in antiques.

The men finished in five days, two of them – not a team – dressed in ordinary work clothes. Almost an anti-climax.

Chas moved everything back on his own and he put it all exactly as he'd found it. Even the fitted carpet was laid immaculately which was amazing as it was old and quite worn. He worked fast and unobtrusively, what a marvel. I wrote to his boss afterwards to praise his work and courteous demeanour. I hope he's been rewarded.

Obviously the work didn't really need doing, but the landlords had no choice but to go ahead after creating such a major to-do, building up the scare factor out of all proportion. I was lucky to have had such strong support from family and friends and of course, Harry, but I'm grateful for inheriting my parents' sense of fair play. Without that I couldn't have withstood the fierce and powerful onslaught.

So all is now quiet inside my flat (outside is another matter) and that must surely be it now. There's nothing left to make an issue out of.

Or is there?

# CHAPTER TWENTY-TWO

I really couldn't think of anything else that the landlords could come up with, but I'm sure that the foot soldiers are already back at the drawing board, not to mention in huddles at the 'Fresh Cut Sandwiches' shelf in the corner shop, plotting the next move. I know the only way for the nightmare to truly end is to leave, but I can't give in now. (I should say here that 'I've been on a life-changing journey', but I would feel like a naff Reality TV contestant). Still, I probably have a couple of months before the next bombshell, so LETS PARTY!

Harry rang from somewhere like The Priory to apologise for not being with me in my hour of need and for asking my solicitor if he was on the landlords' payroll. He said he was going to sail around the world so he wouldn't see me for a while. I told him to keep his feet dry and not go for a walk, however tempting the water looked.

My oldest friend and surrogate brother, Jack Ryder, rang to say he was going up to Bradford and did I want a lift. It seemed a good idea to get away for a few days so I readily accepted. Jack lives in London but has kept his house on the outskirts of the city. On the edge of the glorious moors, I could see why he'd never let go. He can afford it as he is a partner in a successful design company. We'd known each other since school days and had never lost touch. He has never married, although he has a sixteen year old daughter to an ex-partner. He's intelligent and attractive in a Tommy Lee Jones sort of way but we'd never fancied each other, as that would have felt like incest. However, by the way my mother greeted him when we arrived at her place, it was obvious she didn't look on him as a *son*.

"Jack, love, I don't know why our Lily didn't settle down with you, you'd be a *lovely* son-in-law."

"Mother, stop it! Jack and I are not like that. We're best friends, much better."

Jack just laughed as he was used to this familiar banter. Mmm, well... I'd lived too long in the south to appreciate such embarrassing bluntness. Mind you, I had always found Tommy Lee Jones an interesting man...

There wasn't much to do the next day as it was Sunday, so I decided to go to Harrogate as there was an antiques fair in one of the hotels. My mother said she would come with me as long as we didn't go to Betty's Café for lunch. Betty's was the reason *why* most people went to Harrogate (or Ilkley, to its sister branch.) The food was delicious, but admittedly relatively pricey

"We can get a cup of tea and a custard slice just as good in the church. Daft prices to sit and look out on a car park." (Ilkley).

"But we can look out on the Stray at all the beautiful flowers from this one."

"We can sit *on* the Stray and look at the flowers for nothing."

Of course I knew what she meant, but we all need treats, even when we're broke (particularly when we're broke). My mother's idea of a treat was to go out for the day and then go home and settle down with a nice cup of tea – the last bit being the treat.

I liked Harrogate very much; an old Spa town attractively laid out, with an air of grandeur that hadn't diminished despite it being an increasingly expanding conference centre. When we arrived I went straight to the fair, although if there had been any bargains, I thought I would have missed them, as it was in full swing when we got there. I did manage to pick up a 1920's silk Chinese jacket lined with ermine, with silver and jade buttons for £45. (I would later sell this for £250, mainly for the buttons). As I only had about another £80 left to spend on stock, I was almost pleased not to find anything else, as that meant another day of having a purpose on my travels, rather than merely sightseeing. I loved my visits up north, the views, as I've mentioned, were awe-inspiring but it was also fun to pop into far-flung Aladdins' caves and discover treasures – and that can mean anything from a real 'find' to a box of Victorian lace handkerchiefs.

I wanted to buy the Sunday papers, but as it was mid-afternoon, most of the shops were closed.

"You won't get any papers round here," my mother said; a trifle smugly I thought.

"But the Conservative party hold their conferences here. Supposing they want to read about what they've been up to in the News of the World?"

She just laughed, and repeated, "You won't get any."

"Well, what am I supposed to do with myself tonight whilst you're singing hymns with whatshername…Janette Scott's mother, on Songs of Praise?"

"You mean Thora. Thora Hird. Oh, I do like her. Well I don't know, you'll have to read."

Oh, this was so exasperating.

"That's what I'm trying to do! Otherwise I'll have to read your Patience Strong 'Quiet Thoughts For Rainy Days', whatever it's called."

The bus was empty when we boarded so my mother asked the driver if he knew of any paper shops that were open. Her exact words were, "My daughter, up from London, married to Dan Walters, three daughters…" Only joking. She did say that I was up from London though, and used to buying papers late as shops stayed open for twenty four hours there.

"No problem," he said, and stopped the bus a mile or so down the road (nowhere near a bus stop) and waited whilst I bought the papers. Brilliant. Can you imagine a London bus driver doing that?

On the way back through Shipley, I noticed a board outside a café advertising 'Haddock Stuffed With Prawns And Other Things'.

`The following day, Moira, another friend, rang to invite us on a trip into the Dales. I suggested Hawes, as it was not only a picturesque village, the home of Wensleydale cheese, but also the drive there was breathtaking. My mother declined the invitation, saying she would feel sick if she travelled that far (a seventy mile round trip) over bumpy roads, and anyway she didn't like Wensleydale cheese. But what about the stunning views, I asked.

"Well I can't look out of the window if I'm talking to Moira, can I? And I can see hills and gorges, if I want to see them, on Baildon moors."

"Not gorges, you can't."

"Well, they look like gorges from where we sit."

I didn't buy anything from the numerous antiques shops, but it was a lovely day and I really felt that I was back to my old self. I realise that Hawes is now going to be invaded by manic depressives seeking a quick fix and I'm sorry about that, but at least those cheese vats will be working overtime.

My mother was upset when it was time to say goodbye as she looked forward to my infrequent visits. I appear to go often, but I don't really; I could go more. And I will – once I've got my life sorted. I went back via Ilkley as I love that place. It's a steep climb up to the moors but once there, it is so exhilarating. I whizzed round the charity shops as my last twenty pounds was burning a hole in my pocket. I bought a necklace for £3, then immediately regretted it as it was horrible, and would never sell. That waste of money (and I'm talking the price of a sandwich here) bugged me for the rest of the day. I would rather have gone to Betty's and looked at the car park for an hour.

Waiting at the bus station (it would have been quicker to Leeds by train but I preferred the scenic route), a pretty young woman came up to me and asked if I was waiting for the Skipton bus. I replied that I was going to Leeds.

"Do you live there?" she asked. I didn't really want to get into conversation. I have never chatted to strangers, and I didn't want to start now. She obviously wanted to, though.

"I live at Burley, I'm at the hospital. They say I'm a bit schizo, but I think it's just nerves."

I'd better join in, I think.

"Do you work?" she asked next. I nod and shake my head at the same time (it must be catching). She continued, "Have you ever been a nurse?"

"No," I reply, adding stupidly, "Have you?"

"I'd like to be one. I've been a cleaner."

Humouring her, I said, "Perhaps you could become a ward orderly."

She shook her head. "No. But I could become a sister or a matron. I'd be good at telling people off." Then swiftly moving on, she waved at my hair. "I used to have long hair." She moved closer. "I think you get on better in life if you've got long hair. I used to go with someone once with long hair."

Best friends now, she asked me if I bit my nails. I said no, but mentally, I'd just chewed the lot off. We compared nails until my bus came – thankfully my companion was going to Skipton.

"They let me go home during the week, I just go in at weekends."

Surely that's the wrong way round...

"I've got a twin sister," she beamed proudly.

"What, in hospital?"

"Oh no, she's in Skipton."

I wondered if that were true, or was that just the other self talking. We said our fond goodbyes but when I gazed out of the window at her, she looked blankly past me.

I received some terrible news today. Kelly died last night. I knew he was ill with lung cancer, but he hadn't told me how serious it was. Indeed, the last time we spoke, he'd given every indication that the treatment was working. He said I could visit him in a couple of weeks time. What he didn't say was that he was ringing from a hospice in Hastings.

Kelly had moved to Hastings shortly after Dan and I bought our house, as he had fallen in love with the place whilst making a programme about the old town. He was a heavy smoker and there was every chance that he would get lung cancer one day, but not at fifty-four. He knew Dan of course, but out of deference to me he had seen little of him since our split. Also, I understood that Dan was touring extensively again, so he was rarely home anyway.

Marsha wanted to go to the funeral as she had also worked with Kelly in the past, so we travelled together. We took the train as we knew that we would be drowning our sorrows at the wake afterwards. I'd spent days finding the 'right' outfit. I'd trawled the charity shops all over London as I couldn't afford new and anyway Kelly would have thought I was mad to spend more than a tenner on something that would end up covered in tears, coleslaw and draught cider. The black dress I eventually found was perfect; simple but attractive. Discreetly sexy, Kelly would have said. It was one of the hottest days of the year, so I sprayed my straw hat black, stuck a blood-red rose in the brim, and I was ready. I wanted to look good for Kelly (and me an atheist). I also have to be honest; there would be people there I hadn't seen for ages and I wanted to look my best.

We took a taxi from the station and it pulled up outside the crematorium six feet away from DAN. Oh, horror of horrors. I had never thought for one minute that he would be there. I backed out of the cab mouthing to Marsha, "It's Dan. I can't speak to him, can you pay the driver?" I walked swiftly to the other side of the assembled throng, averting my eyes. And that's how I spent the rest of the day, making certain he was as far away as possible, and hiding behind people if he came into my vision. He was with 'her' – his wife now, I'd heard. They didn't look very happy and I noted with satisfaction that they weren't holding hands like we would have been, this was an occasion that called for white knuckle clenches. She looked even dowdier than I remember; her calf length skirt loose and ill-fitting, her blouse matronly and frumpish. I know I looked great compared to her and for a nano second I felt sorry for her. No, sod that. I hoped she knew who I was and felt pea green, and I hoped Dan would look at her in a different light – if he hadn't already. He *must* be wishing he was still with me. Mustn't he?

This was not how I wanted to spend the day, scoring points and dodging behind wilting pot plants. Kelly would have liked it though (he would have also liked the mourner who, on hearing the funeral was at the seaside, brought a swimsuit). I did meet up again with several people, and I was pleased to see them, but I wasn't in the mood to laugh and joke (as one does at funerals), for not only was I missing Kelly, but I was also missing Dan all over again. The only thing to do was get drunk.

Kelly's ex-wife called me over. We'd been friends in the beginning but then she began to suspect that Kelly and I were having an affair as we often worked late together. So can you blame her? I did have a huge crush on Kelly and he had said if he were not married things might have been different, but he took his vows seriously. He also said that if we did get together it would be fantastic for about six weeks, and then it would all fall apart. He was right. We had this love/hate relationship as we were both volatile. I couldn't just shrug when he did things like take one of my tapes, yet to be broadcast, and record something from his car radio over it.

"Where's that exclusive Michael Jackson interview, Kelly? It was here on your desk, on top of your socks."

"Oh, I had to borrow it," he replied casually. "I needed to tape something urgently on my way home."

There must have been two million old tapes around that he could have used but he chose one, clearly labelled, that was not only still to go out, but was also an exclusive interview to boot.

"I might be able to salvage something, I'll listen to it again," trying to fool me that he'd listened to it in the first place. (He usually listened to my interviews just before we recorded the programme). "Don't get so uptight. It's no big deal."

I would then swear at him, sweep his overflowing IN and OUT trays onto the floor (let him sort that lot out), and storm out of the office, slamming the door so loud that people in offices down the corridor would say, "That's Kelly upsetting Lily again." The strops – and there were many – wouldn't last long and then we would be back to the fun-filled relationship that we had together.

Alison had divorced Kelly some years ago (she'd met someone who was temperamentally more suited, let's say), but they'd had a son together, so had remained close. Harvey was now a handsome young man, the image of his attractive mother. He had organised the funeral and was managing to be the perfect host – if that's the right word – and keep his composure at what must have been the most daunting moment of his life. Alison and I greeted each other like long lost friends, which of course we were, the past over and now irrelevant. However, I did feel I owed it to her to lay her fears to rest (what could have been a more appropriate day to do so?) once and for all.

"Kelly and I *never* had an affair. There's nothing to lose now, so if there *had* been anything between us, I could tell you. We had a couple of snogs, and that's all. You were his wife and he never forgot that. I know that he was never at home, but he was just wrapped up in work. I'm sure he never had an affair with *anyone* whilst he was married to you. He was a really decent man – bloody annoying, but really honourable and very special."

I got up from the table and went to the 'powder room' in tears. I know it's allowed and, indeed expected, to weep at funerals but I didn't want Dan to see me and wonder if I were crying over him. I wasn't at that moment. I was in pain at the loss of my dear, dear friend.

Dan and the person he was with got up to go. They had looked awkward and uncomfortable all day and my presence can't have helped. Mind you, Dan must have known that I would be there. I was relieved when they left, but rather than relax with a cup of tea, I knocked back the booze even more. Marsha was doing the same, I noted. At least we would be able to prop each other up. We left at about 8.30 pm and as most of the crowd were from the area, the place was still heaving. As indeed were many of the mourners. When we arrived at the station we were told to go on to Eastbourne to get a connection to London (we were so drunk that if we'd been told to go via Calais we would have done). When we got there, the last train had gone. Ten o'clock on a Saturday night, midsummer, in a popular seaside town, how could this be? We would have to stay.

We must have called in every hotel (some twice, I believe) in Eastbourne before finding one that would take two drunks barely capable of standing. Marsha did the negotiating as several times I got to the desk and then staggered back several paces. She wasn't any more sober than I, but she had managed to cling on to the corners and was hanging on for grim death. She had the cheek to ask for a reduction on the grounds that it was past midnight and it was unlikely that anyone else would turn up now. I don't remember anything after that.

I woke up in unfamiliar surroundings – very grand wherever it was. Marsha was asleep, looking like I felt. I shook her, fearful that we'd checked into a £300 per night luxury hotel – especially as I only had £30 on me (or anywhere, for that matter). Although she felt as rough as I did, her memory was better.

"It was supposed to be ninety, but we got it for fifty. Twenty-five each, that is."

I couldn't believe our luck. The hotel was at the nice end, near Beachy Head, and was elegant and welcoming (we had scrubbed up reasonably well). The £50 included breakfast – amazing, I know. We were ushered into a beautiful dining room and served a five-star gourmet feast by polite, smart waiters. As much as I would like to give publicity to this place, I'm not going to as I would hate it to be overrun the next time I went back.

If only I could have rung Kelly to tell him how things had turned out, then that *would* have been the perfect ending to a most memorable day.

Now that the dust had settled – literally – at the flat, I began to feel apprehensive again. I still didn't know for sure where I stood. The landlords hadn't written to say they couldn't find anything else to do to try and get me out. I know that I have to live for the moment and not worry about the future, but what happens when the 'moment' is utter crap? Is it allowed then to not live for the moment? I'm so confused.

There was a documentary on television earlier which made that moment really worth savouring (spilling over into the next moment, briefly). It was filmed in Blackpool at the local hairdressers and centred on a group of mainly elderly women and their chit-chat. It would have done Alan Bennett proud.

"I only ever sit on the edge of a chair, so I never get much use out of a chair for the money."

"She's very stuck up, she walks about every morning doing nothing."

"I keep a funeral bag in the salon for anyone to borrow. We do have quite a few deaths so it's used a lot. I always put a mint and a hankie in it."

Magic.

Kieran has to go. He came round after the documentary and was pleased to see that I was in a good mood. At first it was fine. He knocked the Tippex bottle over onto a hired video. He suggested that I paint the whole thing white and if I did it carefully, they would never notice. Annoying, but not enough to merit throwing him out. I admit I did moan about Damocles' bloody sword still hanging around, so I suppose it wasn't surprising that he turned on me. But he actually reduced me to tears. He said some horribly hurtful things that were not the sort of things a part-time lover was supposed to say. Thinking about it, it was no doubt the part-time lover bit that was at the root of it. I didn't really want sex with Kieran any more, so it was always a struggle for him to convince me that I did. He resented the rejection, so this was his way of getting back.

Well no more struggling – apart from getting him out of the flat – it was over. I know I've said it before, but I meant it this time.

I took my few new things to Portobello and, surprisingly, I had a good day. Some of my 'dead' stock sold (things at the back that I had long given up on) and one or two more recent things. I don't really want to admit that I sold the horrible necklace that I bought in Ilkley, as I made such a fuss about it (it's not the money, it's the principle), but I did, and made a profit of £5. And that's the beauty of this business, you just never know. I mentioned to a friend, who drops in to say hello every Saturday, that the more you know about antiques, the more you realise how little you know. She replied that an amateur like herself didn't even know how much she didn't know.

A silly, pompous little twit who likes to think of himself as an important dealer was at a stand opposite. Barry has beautiful things, silver and bronzes from various periods. The Twit wanted details of a fine Georgian (silent 'i') mirror.

"Is it Edwardian or George-Ian?" he asked.

Fed up with the fool, Barry replied, "No. I'm afraid that's George Enid."

I hope this business doesn't give me up entirely as I do have fun. Still, today I was rich. I'd taken (not made) £240 after rent so I could pay my NUJ back payments (they were threatening to cast me out), hopefully buy a bit of stock and stretch to a decent bottle of wine for a change. Shopping around threw up loads of bargains and it would be possible to get an £8 bottle of wine for under a fiver. Fingers crossed that my nice day wouldn't be spoiled by a letter from the landlords waiting for me at home (worrying about it was already spoiling it a tad), and luckily there was no post. It would have been nice, though, to have had a friendly letter from someone. Like Ray Davies wanting me to write a musical with him.

In fact, seven more Saturdays went by before 'it' arrived.

'Dear Ms Francis,

We have bent over backwards for you and we are sick and tired of your procrastinations as we really want your flat to do up for a few quid and then sell it to a footballer's wife and her husband for millions. So we have come up with a foolproof way to get you out with all your George Enid furniture.

Very best wishes to you and your family.

Mr & Mrs Landlord.'

This was of course the real meaning of the formal letter written in solicitor speak that was about to trigger a chain of events that would change my life for good.

# CHAPTER TWENTY-THREE

I mentioned earlier that for about two years I had to put up with only a trickle of water in the kitchen, rather than have new sets of pipes installed as not only couldn't I face the disruption, but also I couldn't trust the landlords not to 'discover' something else when it was being done. Work had started on seriously converting the store rooms surrounding me, so life had become even more unbearable (I didn't think it was possible), as the rooms were sledgehammered into bare shells. The communal pipes which ran through my flat and the whole of the basement area were numerous, huge and ugly, like something out of a Fritz Lang film. I could see why they would have to come out of the proposed new flats area, but that would mean disrupting me in order to do this.

The letter stated that I would have to switch over to electricity, as apparently I was the only resident left on the old system and it was no longer a viable proposition to keep the boilers running just for my benefit. Also, they were coming to the end of their life cycle, and therefore it was imperative that I switch over immediately. Naturally the pipes would have to come out, and as that was a major undertaking, I would have to be temporarily re-housed.

I am lost for words. I'll have to go for a walk. See you in a couple of hours.

OK, so this is what I'm going to do. I will appear to co-operate, but the sting will be that rather than have all the disruption, I will be happy to keep the pipes as they can be capped off. Should I ever move, (!!!) then would be the time to rip them out as part of the makeover.

I knew this wouldn't be acceptable but they had to be careful about inconveniencing me for the new conversions and they would never admit to wanting to get me out. I even suggested to Two Hats that work had recently been suspended on the new flats because of the pipes problems. He flatly denied this.

Weeks again dragged by whilst they tried to come up with a solution. There was also a small matter of a fire door that I used (well, hadn't yet, but you never know), which led through a small room into the yard. The room had now been scheduled for conversion and would be part of one of the proposed flats. So what was I supposed to do if there were a fire and the door was bricked up? Hope a passer-by would be carrying a ladder with him on his way to the pub? The building controller who kept his eye on things listened to all the spurious arguments and agreed with me that it was my fire door and as such couldn't be blocked up unless a suitable alternative were found. As that would prove difficult, it appeared I had won round one, thanks to the persistence and close scrutiny of John Slater, the Council's meticulous controller.

Ignoring my suggestion of capping the pipes, another letter finally arrived reiterating how urgent the work was, again emphasising how ancient the boiler was and that work would commence in ten days time. I replied by return (in fact I hand delivered it that same day), stating that I refused to have the work done on their spurious grounds – after all my lease stated that I would be supplied from a central boiler. No get out clause. That would give them another headache as no one had thought to look closely at my lease, it would appear.

My coup de grace – which I was saving – was that I had checked out the boiler room. You see I remember when the current boiler was installed, and it wasn't so many years ago. So I rang the company who installed it and was assured that there were several years yet to go before it would need replacing. Yes! Yes! Yes! I believed I'd got them.

Bastards.

At least it was wonderfully peaceful now, as the work had stopped completely. I couldn't relax though, as I knew they wouldn't give up. And sure enough, a court order was issued against me. I had to get a solicitor. I couldn't go back to the last one as not only had Harry upset him big time, but as no money was involved, he didn't get a penny for the work he did.

So this was it. The denouement. Finally, my day in court. I *so* didn't want to go. I felt confident, sort of, but I might get a judge who liked rich landlords and hated clever clogs (I had been one so far). Oh well, I'm bloody fed up with the whole sodding thing so whatever, bring it on.

I had no choice but to go back to the solicitor I'd turned down when he said he thought I could take care of myself. I hadn't turned him down in so many words; I just never went back. As nearly three years had passed since we met, I hoped he wouldn't remember me – and he'd only looked up once briefly at me anyway. He didn't say if he did or not, but he was still the same world weary off-hand chap. It didn't bode well.

Louis Haynes now held my future in his hands. I had to get on with him, although I knew it was going to be difficult as he showed no interest in my case whatsoever. I signed the usual green form so that we could be up and running immediately. He said I'd have no problem getting legal aid, given my financial situation. At least that was something. He would drop a line to the other side to find out what was going on. I'd just told him, for fuck's sake. He mustn't have listened. Bored to tears. I think on balance (or should that be 'unbalance'), I'd rather have Harry represent me.

Two weeks went by and I'd heard nothing. I couldn't stand the suspense, but I didn't dare call Mr. Haynes as he might shout at me like that other one, 'Your time is up; don't call me again.' Actually, he wouldn't shout it, he'd yawn it at me.

Well, well. Louis Haynes, what a dark horse. I thought my letters to the landlords were sarcastic, but his was a masterpiece in subtle contempt. I think I'm in love.

And now, at last, a good night's sleep.

Over the weeks that followed we had several meetings as the other side took ages to reply to Louis, and even he said that he'd never known anyone take so long. He also thought they were quite off-hand. That from Louis, who was still apparently bored with my case and made no effort to reassure me in person that I stood a chance of winning. However, his letters were consistently something else, and I knew that I'd struck gold. I hoped it was only a matter of time before he would admit that he did find my case interesting – or how else could he have written those brilliant letters? – and so I was happy to go along with his strange charade. I presumed that it was something he did with everyone regardless of what he thought their chances were.

Finally the letter we were waiting for arrived. Despite all the attempts to dissuade them, the landlords had decided to go to court.

Louis didn't seem particularly fazed by this, and even said he thought we might win. That was such a boost, to hear him so positive, that I was almost excited now about 'the big day'.

Louis said it was more than likely the other side would attempt to settle before the hearing. Just before the hearing, half an hour before in fact. I couldn't believe that I was 'tackled' by their barrister – who didn't seem that familiar with the case – and someone to do with the construction of the proposed new flats. They hadn't a clue really. and I told them that they'd got their facts wrong and no, I wouldn't do a deal, I would rather let the judge decide.

My barrister was not only swooningly handsome, but also, in the short time that he'd had to familiarise himself with the case, he had a good all round grasp of it. The judge asked pertinent questions and both sides gave their answers, mine succinctly and politely. The other side were not able to answer several of the straight forward queries and got a ticking off for not being prepared. At one point, the judge said he didn't believe that the landlords could change my lease to now include a clause about the boiler not being kept. (I *thought* I was right on that one).

It was a relatively short hearing as the judge wasn't presented with all the facts, so basically I won that round, the other side being ordered back to the drawing board. We were awarded costs (I hope they were astronomical) and that was that. Louis thought the time was now right to invite the landlords to settle once and for all.

The reply was swift (a first) and to the point (also a first). Yes, they would settle at my price.

It was a fantastic result, but the money hadn't come easily – nightmare years – and I would have to move away from the area that I loved, as even one-bedroom flats were more than my settlement (I hadn't been greedy; indeed, I was advised all along the way to ask for more). But justice had been done, with the help of some like-minded, wonderful people.

Hello? Louis? Well, thank you very much, I'd love to. But why don't you come here instead? I haven't cooked a decent meal for ages. You're not a vegetarian by any chance? Good. Neither am I.